D1519444

Lightning Crashes

T. James White

Books by T. James White

Lightning Crashes
(Angels of War Chronicles)

Wine in the Sand
(My Adventures through Desert Storm)
Written as Jim White

To the best person to be trapped in a
foxhole with.
Mary

Acknowledgements

I am indebted and eternally grateful to my
editor Julie Dunn Crawford. I wasn't sure
anyone would read this book even once, and
she has sifted through my mangled words
from beginning to end more times than
Mulder and Scully have flicked on a
flashlight. Thanks for taking my ramblings
and molding them into an acceptable tale.

Have you seen that cover? It certainly didn't
start out that way. Karen Minzner listened to
my crazy ideas for months, but finally the
right balance was found and she was able to
use her magic and turn my concept into
reality. With the help of Liz Knochelmann,
this is beyond my best hopes. Thank you
both.

FORWARD

After reading this book, my best advice to someone like you (a person contemplating reading this rag of lies) is to rethink your life choices. Put this down and walk away. If you are lucky, maybe no one saw you holding it in the first place. No good could possibly come from reading this trash. Not a word of it is true. Zero. Nada. What lies within these pages is the unhinged ramblings of someone who is clearly in need of multiple strong medications. The word "delusional" comes to mind, but that doesn't begin to lick at the tip of this titanic sinking iceberg. This will be a waste of your time and money. You've thusly been warned and I now bear no responsibility for the corruption of your common sense.

Carl G. Busch

1

Murder? Nah.

I never enjoyed killing someone. Even when they deserved it, I never felt good afterward. Today was no different. As hard as I had tried to not kill this idiot, he just wouldn't get out of his own way. Normally, I wouldn't put this much effort into avoiding taking someone out. Time is a factor and if someone didn't take my gift of life the first time I offered it, then the outcome is on them. I almost always give someone at least one chance, unless it's a 'them or me' situation. Then it's them. It has to be. I'm on a mission from GOD. I've always wanted to write that! It's my favorite line from *Blues Brothers*, but in this case, it's true. Kind of true. The Big Man Himself (ITSELF - it's complicated) made it clear to his team what had to be done. So, here I am, removing this dipstick in front of me so I can get on with my mission.

I was currently pointing my favorite Glock 23 (the one with the custom-made silencer) at Mr. Lloyd. I made the addition myself, fewer paper trails and questions that way. When you're trying to save humanity, too many questions can slow you down. Hence, the deadly situation Mr. Lloyd currently found himself in. I had given Mr. Steve Lloyd, his one chance to amscray three weeks ago but he obviously didn't believe my threat/promise. Back in Kentucky, I told him in no uncertain terms if he refused to stop his homespun investigation, he was going to put his personal goals on hold for many lifetimes to come. I was purposely being ambiguous in hopes that he would mull it over and drop this spy hobby. Unfortunately, he was pretty good at being a self-taught Sherlock but that only got him so far. He now found himself in far more trouble than he could have ever anticipated.

"Look," he said, as he tried to act brave, "I know who you are and what you're trying to do. If you let me go now, I promise not to kill you." Poor Steve. He wasn't doing himself any favors by threatening the guy holding the gun. From the outside, I'm sure Steve-O believed he had very cleverly discovered and followed an invader from another country, hell-bent on destroying the United States. In that much, I was successful, because if he knew the actual truth, there would be little trouble. No one, absolutely NO ONE would believe my actual mission but I still had to cover my tracks. Either way, I was engaging in some pretty lawless behavior, and no matter my reasons, if I were caught, it would certainly slow me down. I had no need for publicity or television cameras or courtrooms, and especially not prison.

Prison can *really* slow you down. Been there, learned that. Never again.

The only reason he didn't have a few extra holes in him already was because I wanted to be sure there were no witnesses within earshot. It was doubtful. I had led Steve several miles away from the main town of Leadville, into an area of long-abandoned mines. No city lights, only stars. You could see a car approaching from any direction for miles. Perfect for dispatching pesky "Steves." How crazy was this guy to follow someone into the wilderness of a long-abandoned mining quarry at 2:00 AM? Didn't Steve ever watch Scooby-Doo? He was just asking for trouble. He found it. Again.

One more glance around to be sure then I offered this last bit of advice.

"Steve, listen closely. When you cross over, I want you to think long and hard about the stupidity of what you just did. You could have gone on and been a productive individual and worked out some of your problems, but you let yourself get sidetracked. I'm sure your teachers will help you with this incessant need to put your nose in places it has no business sticking."

"WAIT! WAIT! What are you talking about!?" Steve practically screamed. "You'll never get away with this! The others know where I am! They will come looking for me!"

"One last thing, Steve," I offered. "Make sure you don't get in my way again." Hopefully, by the time he would have that opportunity, my mission will be over.

Steve opened his mouth to argue but I pulled the trigger. Silencers aren't truly silent. They make a very distinct sound, but in this case, it did the job. Only if you were within thirty yards would you have heard the slightest noise. Since no one was within miles of us, the deed was well concealed. Steve's head jerked as he stumbled backward, falling onto the rocks that littered the ground, tons and tons of discarded stone pulled out of the earth by miners so many years ago. I hoped his team was watching carefully and had pulled him out before the lead actually blasted into his brain, but that wasn't my call. Steve was now in for some embarrassing self-reflection and the realization he derailed his own agenda. It certainly wasn't the first time this had happened, but eventually, it would have to end. I was becoming an expert at dispatching souls who had lost their way and it wasn't something of which I was particularly proud. Efficiency doesn't always breed gratification.

I grabbed Steve's body and dragged it the few feet needed to drop it into the long empty mine shaft. At just over 10,000 feet altitude, it was chilly in the evenings so I didn't work up much of a sweat, even though it was mid-August. The air was crisp and sound seemed to travel farther here, or maybe I was just used to all of the trucks and aircraft sounds back home. Judging from the time I heard the final thud, Steve's body was now some 100 or more feet underground. When and if his remains were ever found, I'd be long gone from Leadville, and maybe even Earth itself.

There was nothing particularly special about this Glock except for the silencer modification I'd made. I could do that to any Glock so losing this particular one wasn't a big deal. I really didn't want to make another silencer though. I'd put the time and effort into making this one and didn't relish having to do it again. I disassembled the gun and threw the parts into three different abandoned mine pits. I took the silencer and buried it under a pile of rocks. Keeping evidence so soon after an incident was never a wise idea. I'd try to come back to retrieve it later but if not, I wouldn't lose any sleep over it.

I had come to this town to meet my team and finish up a mission. My cover story of being here to run the Leadville 100 ultramarathon was perfect. It gave me a week by myself to acclimate to the altitude while actually tracking down exactly where the ship was buried. The rest of my crew were scheduled to meet me tomorrow after I had secured our house and gathered our supplies. Steve tried to throw a wrench into our affairs. Hopefully, no one would actually come looking for

Mr. Lloyd. We'd cross that bridge when and if we came to it. Now I had to drive Steve's car to Aspen, use his credit card in a few places to leave a Steve trail, and then find my way back to Leadville.

Getting to this point has taken a long time. A *long, long* time. There have been several "Steves" along the way. But to understand how it came to this, we have to start in a much different place, in a much different time. You will probably have to suspend your entire belief system to read this story, because what you are about to hear is the truth. I'm not going to sugar coat it for you, which will make it all the more likely you will disregard this as some crazy tale. The truth is complicated and the lies you have been told are easy to digest. Most people don't want to have to connect the dots and do the hard work. If someone is willing to spoon-feed you some easily believable facts then that's the picnic that most people gobble up. That's exactly what the enemy has always used to control us. It has always worked, not only on an individual scale, but on a global one as well.

That's where my mission comes in. I know the truth. I've been sent here to save humanity and I've been given full authority to do anything and everything possible to succeed. Even dispatching the occasional Steve is well within my parameters. If that sounds a bit heavy-handed, you need to understand how this really works. Being fed a history of lies your entire life, no one wants to admit to being duped that severely. Not a person, not a group of scientists, not a society and not an entire planet; *especially* not the world's religions. But if the lie was started from the very beginning and built into the very fabric of your existence, with carefully planted truths seeded along the way then you'd look like a fool not to believe them. Hell, I'd believe them, too, if I were you. But I'm not. I have the burden, or the luxury, of full knowledge of all of the lies, how they were doled out and gobbled up, and why it was done. In a single word: **control**. You are controlled by your knowledge, or what you believe is the truth. Even after I lay this out for you, in no uncertain terms, most of you will refuse to believe it. That's okay. Some of you will believe and we will be the ones to protect the doubters. Some of you already suspect the truth but with only a tidbit here and a half-truth there, you only know enough of the story to be a pesky insect to be swatted away. Strap in, pay attention and take notes as I explain how this all started, over six thousand years ago.

2

In My Beginning

*T*hroughout history, humans have debated *when the beginning of life is.* Is it at three months in the womb? Six months? When you pop out of your dear ol' mom or at that first breath? Maybe it's when you can detect a heartbeat. When they found out about cells and how they divided after Mr. Sperm invaded Ms. Egg, we had more to think about. Life. It's meaning and its beginning is a debate that has never ceased to be a moving target. Unless you are just discussing when enough cells divide enough times to be an organism, then it's moot. A sperm is an organism in itself. So, be careful when you skip down this road of knowledge. It's a slippery slope. Maybe *life form* is a better debate? Good luck with that one, too. It seems that, depending on your agenda, this changes as the winds blow and the tides roll in and out. This is entirely a human debate. Souls are another matter completely, and it's very cut and dry. It's so clear, it's practically boring. To understand all of this, I'll use my beginning as an example.

The Creator's most well-known and clear job is creating. Duh, right? But through no fault of their own, humans have been given the story wrong. Well, mostly wrong. While we are all fairly certain the Creator gave the universe its existence, He (It?) has never told anyone that information. Even the oldest of us don't know this for certain. (I'm going with "He" from here on out; it's just easier that way, but in absolutely no terms should you infer that the Creator has a gender. He has never given anyone any impression that He prefers a gender, and truthfully, He has so many other options beyond male and female that it becomes a ridiculous debate. Humanity has been calling the Creator a "He" for so long, it's just easier to tell you the story this way. Feel free to insert any adjective for the Creator that makes you feel warm and fuzzy. He will not be offended. Frankly, as far as we know, He doesn't care) We simply know that He was the first one here, so it has always stood to reason that He created it. What we are absolutely certain of is that he created us. Each and every individual soul was made by Him. That alone sounds like a miracle, right? So, as far as the debate goes for someone's beginning, souls, as a group, know their beginning to be the instant the Creator turned them into something - a soul - from nothing. We were nothing and then we were something. The entire discussion as to when we became human is a non-issue for souls. Zero. Once we were created, we began, and when we enter or leave a human isn't as important as what we do while we're in the human, but I'm getting ahead of myself.

White light. Warmth. Love. Those are my very first memories. I had no sense of time or space or anything. I just was. I could have been in this state for an hour or a thousand earth years. There was nothing to gauge existence against. I was happy, I knew that. Eventually, I also began to feel the presence of others around me. I knew they loved me and were somehow taking care of me. Then, sometime later, there were sounds, like distant chimes and hums. It became my focus. It was the apex of soothing. Much, much later, I found out this place was called the nursery. Perfectly fitting. How souls refer to their time in this space is oddly similar to how they refer to things when they are in human form. There are plenty of other forms, and maybe our shared thoughts just come across that way, but nursery is how I hear it in my head. I could have existed like this forever but there were other plans for me. Big, Earth-saving plans.

3

PLAN B

There is always a Plan A. I don't always have a Plan B, but if necessary, I'll make one up on the spot. After dumping Steve down the hole, I was now officially on Plan B. I was formulating it on the move. I didn't have to be back in Leadville to meet the team until 11:00 tomorrow morning so I had plenty of time. I had rented the top floor of a house while staying in town and the caretakers didn't keep track of my coming and going so my future alibi was firmly intact. In fact, my cell phone with its location services was sitting on my bed at the house so if anyone ever cared to check, that is where I appeared to be. Steve may have been an excellent sleuth, but he may have been missing the common sense gene that comes in very handy now and then. Earlier, I had strapped on my running shoes and started out for a late-night run. Perfectly normal for a guy who's about to run a 100 mile race over thirty hours. However, Mr. Lloyd was decidedly not a runner but he somehow believed he could follow me in his car if he kept a discreet distance. The problem was, Steve didn't take into account that I was going to run to the edge of the town and then down several dirt roads, into the middle of nowhere. I had my handy, dandy headlamp to light my way and to give Steve an indication of where I was in the distance. Unfortunately for him, he was forced to use his headlights on this heavily pockmarked dirt road, and could easily be seen for miles away. I felt bad for Steve, just a little. He eventually had to get that feeling in the pit of his stomach that he was making a terrible mistake, but he chose to ignore it and keep on driving, straight to his undoing. Too many people ignore this feeling and it usually ends badly for them.

Now I was in Steve's car driving to Aspen. I'd never been to Aspen. Funny but typical way for me to visit for the first time. This was a 2 ½ hour drive, one way, and since there was little traffic at this time of night, it was unlikely I'd encounter many obstacles to slow me down. The trip back was going to be part of Plan B that I hadn't devised yet. That's okay, I'm good on the fly. The trip was completely uneventful, just the way I like it. Despite the extreme existence I've had, when things go quietly and according to plan, I'm much happier. I do love a good rush of adrenaline now and then, but it's not mandatory, especially when I'm already off script.

I pulled into town just in time to see the *Open* sign on the Aspen Hickory House flicker on. It had been a long night of killing idiots and driving unnecessary miles and I was starving. What better place to use Steve's credit card? As I pulled into the back lot, I did a quick surveillance to ensure there were no obvious, pesky cameras pointed in my direction. Steve had left his Carhartt jacket in the back seat of his rental so with that thrown over my long-sleeved running shirt, and my hat pulled down low, I became perfectly nondescript. There was absolutely nothing outstanding or remarkable worth remembering about me to anyone who cared to notice.

I walked around to the front of the rustic looking wooden building. The painted sign above the front door read "BEST RIBS IN COLORADO". I hoped they had a good breakfast menu too. I reached for the door handle just as a young girl was opening the door. She was wearing a black shirt with a name tag that read "Cindy".

"Come on in, honey. Sit anywhere ya like. You're our first customer of the day," Cindy said with the enthusiasm of someone on their second cup of coffee.

"Good morning," I said. "I can smell the bacon and coffee already so I must be at the right place."

"You sure are, honey. Just make yourself at home and I'll be right over to get your order," she said.

The Aspen Hickory House was just as rustic on the inside as it was on the outside. Wooden tables, chairs and panels on the walls. Skis, sleds, snowshoes and pictures of the mountains hung on every wall as well as from the ceiling. This place must be packed during the ski season, I thought. I was happy it was the off-season and I would probably be leaving before the morning breakfast crowd arrived.

Cindy finished opening the doors and came to my table with a fresh pot of coffee.

"Coffee, hon?" she asked.

"Absolutely, and I'm ready to order when you are," I said.

Cindy fished a paper pad out of her back pocket and pulled a pen from behind her ear. I ordered a western omelet, two pancakes, crispy bacon, and biscuits with gravy. I didn't want to stop again until I made my way back to Leadville so this had to hold me for the next several hours. While I was waiting for Cindy to bring my order, I was finally able to sit back for a moment, relax my brain, and think. How was I going to get back to Leadville? Rent a car and drive back but that would require IDs and insurance and returns; too complicated. Steal a car? I liked that option but it added a degree of danger and unnecessary excitement that I didn't need at the moment. Fly? Was that even an option? I knew Aspen had a small airport, just from hearing stories of the rich and famous flying here to ski, but did Leadville? One way to find out. Cindy returned with my plates, and as she was setting them down, I asked, "Does Aspen have a library?"

Cindy replied, "We sure do, honey. The Pitkin County Library is about nine blocks straight down Main Street and one block to your left. "

"Perfect," I replied.

I did my best to finish every crumb on my plate and paid using Steve's credit card. Steve left an enormous tip for Cindy because she was so prompt bringing coffee refills and her smile seemed genuine, not plastered on her face. Maybe that happened after the lunch rush. I gathered my/Steve's jacket and walked back to the car, just for a quick once-over. I had taken a few extra hand wipes and napkins from the restaurant. They seemed to work well for wiping down steering wheels, door handles and such. No sense making it easy for whoever eventually finds Steve's rental and wants to investigate further. Satisfied that I didn't leave anything behind, I began to walk to the library. Along the way, I ditched the Carhartt into a street trash can. In my running clothes again, I looked like just another runner out for a morning trot around beautiful Aspen. Absolutely nothing to distinguish me from anyone else on the sidewalks.

The sun had risen far enough to peek through the mountain passes so I pulled out my sunglasses and became even less noticeable. I walked the nine blocks, just to take in the views from the street. I've been to nearly every corner of the globe multiple times but when I find a city I haven't visited yet, I try to soak it up. I love this planet and all it has to offer and try to experience all its many wonders, every chance I get. Even when ditching a dead guy's car in a city surrounded by the mountains of Colorado.

One block over and I found the library. I sauntered in as if I had been here a hundred times. Blending in was one of my abilities. I picked this look for that specific reason. Average height, not attractive, but not unattractive. Hazel eyes, brown hair. I just don't stand out in a crowd. Perfect for my mission. I saw the computer area as soon as I walked in but instead of making a beeline, I took my time and walked through some of the stacks, just to get an idea of my surroundings. I was pretty sure no one following me, or Steve's car, but one can't be too careful with so much at stake. I've played this game multiple times now and I'm very good at it.

Satisfied that everything looked normal, I made my way to the front desk. A woman behind the counter, whose name tag read "Carol" greeted me with a smile. "Can I help you?" she asked. I had already seen the sign on the counter which read,

"Computer time free with ID". Steve and I looked nothing alike so there was no using his license. I immediately concocted my story.

"Carol, I'm in a bit of a predicament. I lost my wallet last night and I need to use a computer to contact my credit card companies to turn them off. Is there any way I can use your computer for a few minutes?"

Carol came to my rescue, "I'm *so* sorry!" she said in her best sympathetic voice. "Of course you can. Just pick any open computer."

"Thank you *so* much, Carol. I won't be very long, I hope," I said, and with that, I gave her my best sad smile and found the computer farthest away from prying eyes.

I pulled up Google Maps to get an idea where my nearest airport was. Aspen Pitkin County Airport was 3.9 miles away. Excellent! Now for Leadville. I scrolled the map to the right and zoomed in on the city. Lucky again! Leadville-Lake County Airport was just to the southwest of downtown Leadville, barely 3.5 miles from the house I had rented. Some days are luckier than others. Now, if I can keep this streak going, I can find a pilot who needs money more than time to give me a quick hop over the mountain. As the crow flies, it's a 28 mile trip, just a short roller coaster ride. Time to spin the lottery wheel again.

No sense in putting more eyes on me than necessary, I took the next 35 minutes and ran to the airport. Coming down the road, I expected to see the same crappy airport structure which usually greets me at most destinations in the United States. Instead, the airport looked like a glorified, wilderness rest stop beside some woodland interstate. Very nice. Hopefully, the people inside were as laidback as their outward architecture suggested.

As I walked in the front door, I could tell I was in the wrong place. This looked commercial and I needed something a bit more discreet. Hopefully, someone could point me in the right direction. Not wanting to gather undue attention, I stood back and watched for a few minutes. Presto! Just who I was looking for. A ramp worker on a break, grabbing a bite at the little Aspen Marketplace. He looked tired but not unapproachable. Dressed in my running clothes, I appeared a bit out of place, but not overly.

"Excuse me," I said, "Can you answer a quick question for me?"

"Sure," he said, "but I'm just a ramp agent. I don't know anything about ticketing or that end of the airport."

"That's cool," I said, trying to keep this very casual. "Is there a part of the airport where a person can rent the services of a private plane and pilot?"

"Yeah," he said, as he looked north through the building as if the far wall wasn't there. "Just go back out the front of the main building, take a left, and head a few hundred yards. Look for a sign that says Atlantic Aviation. You might find someone in there who can help you."

"Thanks, man," I said, "Can I buy you breakfast?"

"Naw, I'm good, buddy. Good luck," he said

"Thanks," I said, and headed back outside. It was just after 9am. If all went smoothly, I'd be back just in time to meet the team. If all went smoothly. When did that ever happen?

4

I'm Me

*O*ne day, while enjoying the hums and chimes and tones, I felt a different presence. Suddenly, where there had been only a white hazy pattern around me, other shapes began to appear, and with it, colors. I didn't know what any of this meant, but it was an interesting change in my existence and this made me happy. Next, there was a blue shape approaching me, and I heard a voice. (I only know the color blue now. At the time, I had no concept of color, or what it might possibly mean. Color was just a different shade of something other than the thing next to it.)

"Hello, little one, I'm Morah, and I'm going to be your teacher," it said. Morah's voice made me feel very safe. There was almost a melody to it. "You will have many names but here you will be called Timlis."

Timlis. That sounded fine with me. Actually, everything sounded fine. Every single thing that happened was new and that was interesting and exciting. I had no concept of who or what I was, or even where I was. None of that seemed to matter. I had a name, I had a teacher and I felt loved.

Since I knew of nothing else, I didn't know to even wish this would never stop. I just was, and that was all I knew.

"We have much to teach you, Timlis. For now, all you need to know is that you are a special soul and that you are at the beginning of the greatest adventure any soul has ever undertaken. You have much to learn, but we will get to that when you are ready."

I didn't even know how to communicate properly, but Morah seemed able to feel what my tiny little thoughts were.

"I can feel how anxious you are to begin, but all in due time. We will begin your education soon. Relax, Timlis. Relax." And with that, Morah's light drifted slowly away and once again, I fell into a state of warmth and love, but now I had thoughts that began to form. I am a soul. Morah is a teacher. I am beginning a great adventure. What did any of this mean? I would not have to wait long to discover the answers.

5

Wheel and Deal

I found Atlantic Aviation easily enough. I walked through the front door and had to do a double-take to make sure I was at the right spot. The inside looked like the lobby of a wilderness hotel lodge, not some tiny private airport. Lots of wood beams. A fireplace. Stonework placed here and there. I guess if you're a jet-setting rich person (technically, I was a jet-setting rich person, but a very, very discreet one), you wanted to be pampered. There was no one at the front desk, so I wandered around until I found someone at the little Carrenos Café and Grill. It was just a window in the wall and a menu posted next to it but it seemed to cover most needs, and just like all other airports, the prices were twice anywhere else. But that wasn't my concern.

A 30-something woman was behind the counter, looking intently at the screen on her phone.

"Hello," I said, which apparently made her jump just a bit. "I need some help."

"Hi," she said, putting her phone into her back pocket. "Can I get you something to eat or drink?"

"Oh, no thanks. I'm actually looking for a ride. I was hoping someone could point me to a pilot who could give me a quick trip. Is there anyone around here that fits that bill?"

"I'm not really sure," she said. "Some guys are out on the ramp talking. You're welcome to go out and ask around. We're pretty laidback here. Just stay clear of the taxiway. Good luck."

"That's great, thanks," I said

I walked out and looked left and right. There were a few smaller jets to my left. Not something I was really looking for. A bit too large for this particular trip. To my right was an assortment of medium and smaller planes. Some were jets, some were prop. Five or six men were standing around one of the smaller jets. It was having some maintenance to one of its engines, as the cowling was off. I walked over, trying to guess who was who. The guy with the wrench in his hand was obviously the guy working on the engine. The rest of the men were laughing at a joke someone had just told. They all stopped laughing as they turned and watched me approach.

"Good morning," I said, in my best out-of-town, friendly voice. "The lady inside said one of you guys might be able to help me or point me in the right direction." No one volunteered to begin speaking so I just keep talking. "I was needing a quick hop over to Leadville and hoped there was someone around who could fly me over."

The guy with the wrench went back to work but talked over his shoulder as he continued to work, "Buddy, that's just over a two-hour drive from here. Wouldn't it be cheaper just to rent a car and drive?"

"I suppose so," I said, staying as cheerful as possible. "But I'd love to see the mountains from the air and visit Leadville, so why not kill two birds with one stone?" I was trying to not look suspicious or appear disrespectful, which I thought I was pulling off pretty well.

"Buddy, that's an awfully expensive trip for such a short flight," the guy with the wrench said.

"Yeah, but I have some cash from Vegas I just won and am looking to burn through it before I get home and the wife just takes it for a shopping spree. This sounds like a fun way to get rid of it," I said with a smile on my face.

That got a good laugh from the crew.

Wrench guy piped up, "If ya walk down about a hundred yards to the hangars, I think Sid is down there, finishing up work on the Cessna. You might be able to catch a ride. Tell Sid that Dwayne sent ya down." Then he pointed north towards the hangers and a long line of smaller planes sitting just off the taxiway.

"Thanks," I said with a smile, and then started walking. The sun was well on the rise and even though it was August, at 8,000 feet it was chilly. It would probably get in the mid-70s today, but right now it was still in the high 40s. If felt good to get some heat going from a quick walk. The guys behind me must have had another joke, probably at my expense, because there was a round of laughter again soon after I departed. Who could blame them? Some guy dressed in running gear asking for an expensive plane ride to cover up a gambling windfall? The joke practically writes itself. I certainly didn't take offense. My entire story was a lie, so I gave them their laugh and maybe had a quick chuckle at myself.

As I approached the planes, sure enough, I saw a figure closing up a tool kit and picking it up to walk back towards the hangers.

"Excuse me!" I shouted before they got too far away from their plane. "Are you Sid?"
As the guy turned around, he took off his ball cap and a mound of brown, curly hair fell over his shoulders, and he suddenly turned into she. Sydney?

"Yeah," she said, "Who's asking?"

Trying for a quick recovery, I said, "Uh, Dwayne said you might be down here finishing up. I was looking for a quick ride to Leadville and was hoping you had time to take me."

"Nope," she said. "I'm just finishing up here and have to meet some people in a few minutes."

"Crap!" I said. "Is there any way $1500 can postpone your meeting? I'm kind of in a pinch and money is really no object. I'd give you more but that's all I have in my pocket. If I have a trusting face, I can Paypal you another thousand when I get to a computer."

She just stopped and looked at me like I was an idiot. I knew this because it's not the first time a woman has looked at me that way. If I live past tomorrow, I'm pretty sure it won't be the last time either. She bent down and set her toolbox on the ground, stood back up, and put her hands on her hips.

"Let me get this straight," she said, "you want me to fly you to Leadville for twenty-five hundred bucks? You do realize that it's barely over a 15-minute flight, right?"

She stood there waiting for me to answer. "May I call you Sid?" I asked, but she just looked at me. Didn't she believe me? I knew I was dressed kind of strangely. I reached into my zippered pocket and pulled out the cash I had stuffed in that pocket the night before. Crazy as it may sound, I try to carry as much cash as possible for situations just like this. Over many, many years, I'd learned that cash money makes people behave differently and gets things done much quicker. Except when wearing swimming attire, I'll nearly always put at least a thousand dollars in my pocket. One-hundred dollar bills don't take up that much room.

She didn't immediately answer so I continued, "Sid, I didn't just rob a blank or anything. I have to meet some people back in Leadville fairly soon and I'd rather be there sooner than later. I have the cash right here and it's yours if we can get in the air in the next fifteen minutes, otherwise, could you point me to someone who could use a few thousand bucks?"

I saw the change in her eyes. She relaxed just a bit and looked back and forth, then back at me.

"Okay, mister," she said, "let me take these tools back to the hangar and grab my stuff. I'll meet you right back here in ten minutes. Should I even ask your name?"

"Thanks! And sure, my name is Jeff." No sense in giving her my real name. This wasn't a relationship and I wasn't trying to leave a trail for anyone's later questions. The less Sid knew, the better. She walked off at a good pace as she put the phone to her ear, presumably calling whoever she was going to meet and cancel.

This gave me a chance to look at my taxi ride. It was a blue and white, twin-engine Cessna 414A. Not only had I been in one of these before but I had owned one some years ago. It held up to two crew, but only needed one, and as many as eight passengers. It had a range of over 1,500 miles and could go 270mph on a good day. It was more aircraft than I needed but that was fine. Better too much than barely enough. For being a plane over thirty years old, it looked practically brand new. Sid apparently took pride in her bird and kept it highly maintained. Maybe she flew corporate and needed to compete with the big dogs. An attractive woman pilot and a perfectly maintained aircraft probably didn't hurt her business model. Plus, she was her own mechanic, so that came in handy when it was time to pay the bills.

Sid came walking back towards me and the aircraft, this time with a well worn, brown leather jacket pulled on, over what looked like an older, military-type flight suit, as well as some paperwork in her hand.

"We have some weather coming in over the mountains so the sooner we take off, the better," she said. She immediately boarded through the door behind the wing, not asking for me to follow her. I took a couple of steps up and looked inside. It didn't have the new plane smell anymore, but it did have a nice old leather vibe going on. She waited at the rear of the plane for me to enter, then she shut the door behind us.

"You're the only passenger today, so take your pick of the seats. Give me a few minutes to get the engines started and our clearance from the tower and we'll be on our way. I'd tell you to just relax but we'll be in Leadville barely before you could get your shoes off and back on again."

"If you don't mind, I'd like to sit up front with you," I asked. She seemed to consider this for a couple of extra seconds.

"Have you ever sat in the cockpit of a plane before?" she asked.

"Yeah, a few times," I lied. I didn't see the need to tell her that I could easily fly this and nearly every other plane on the planet. Less information is better in this case.

"Well, okay then, but you'd be much more comfortable back here. Way more room to stretch out."

"That's okay," I said, "and besides, like you said, there won't be much time to get comfortable anyhow."

"True," she said, as she climbed into the captain's seat on the left. I carefully made my way to the seat on the right. Looking at the controls, I noticed they looked used, but not overly worn. Someone takes very good care of this aircraft. Trying to sound like a newbie, I asked, "Is this a new plane? It hardly looks like it's been used?" That gave her a laugh and a smile. "Ha! No, this plane is thirty-five years old. I just keep her in top shape. Fewer issues that way. Easier to keep it up than catch it up. It's also easier to attract customers with a well-maintained aircraft than one that looks like it might not make it to the end of the runway."

"I've seen cars that are five years old that are in worse shape than what this looks like," I told her. I wasn't kidding. There was no real need to butter her up or stroke her ego but I also didn't like to burn potential bridges. Our paths would probably never cross again but sometimes those lottery numbers swing around and you've got to be ready with they do.

"Okay, put your seatbelt on while I get things going," she said. She put on her own seatbelt and I made a show of watching how she did it so I knew how to follow the leader. She put on her headset and began speaking softly into the mic. I supposed she was talking to the tower, making her intentions known. You can't just go flying off, willy nilly without a flight plan. Well, let me take that back. You *can* go flying willy nilly, but you immediately get lots of attention, and usually not in a good way. You also stop flying airplanes as a career, since your license is promptly shredded. Why do I know this? I've had some experience in these matters.

The engines came to life one at a time and she motioned for me to put on the headset that was hanging on the panel. I slipped it over my run hat and the engine sounds were immediately muffled. She spoke into her mic and I immediately heard her in my ear, "If you want to talk to me, all you have to do is speak. The mics are hot and always on," she said. "10-4," I said with a smile. That remark got me an eye-roll.

I could now hear the tower in my ear, giving her clearance to taxi to the runway. We began moving forward as she steered the aircraft to the taxiway, making her way to the end of the runway. This runway ran a few degrees from true north/south. We taxied to the far south end and turned right onto the runway. There was no other traffic but us. She waited for a few seconds before being cleared and we moved forward at an impressive clip as she pushed the throttles forward to full power. We used just half the runway before we were airborne and gaining altitude quickly. It was going to be a short ride, but as we had a mountain to clear, not a boring one. Up, up, up, and away.

6

It Begins

"Timlis, it is time to begin your education." *It was the voice of Morah.* Up until now, it was the only voice I knew. Looking back, I can tell you he sounded like a wise, even-tempered, ever patient being. Every soul presents the image that it wants you to see. Sometimes it's a person who you remember from a life on Earth. But today, he looked like himself, in his most perfect and natural form, an orb of energy. His color was a deep blue, with other colors on the edges. Much later in my teachings, I would find out what a soul's color signified, but for now, he just seemed like a beautiful color that made sounds inside of me that I could understand. Remember, I was practically an infant soul, so I really didn't have much to go on here.

"What will I learn, Morah?" I asked.

"Everything."

7

Shit Storm

As the Cessna began to climb, we started a slow turn to the right, heading east towards Leadville. We had some tall mountains to fly over, but because we were already at 8,000 feet, they really weren't that tall, relatively speaking. It was a beautiful day to be airborne and for a moment, I could let my mind wander and forget there were people out there full of bad intentions, hoping I would fail in my mission. You can only eat the elephant one bite at a time, so no sense overthinking this. There was a plan, and for the most part, everything was still on schedule. Sid confirmed her heading and instructions with air traffic control and made a few adjustments to her instruments.

"How ya doing?" she asked.

"Just enjoying the view," I said. She smiled back.

"Yeah, this never gets old. Sorry you won't be up here long enough…."

And then she pulled the plane violently to the left as she saw an object come up next to us on the right side. It came from behind us as if we were standing still and then it just stopped and held its place ten feet off our wing. It was a silver, egg-shaped object, with the smaller part of the egg facing forward. No lights. No windows. No visible engines. I'd seen this once before, and instantly knew what was about to happen.

Sid threw the plane to the left again and made a series of quick maneuvers as she attempted to put some distance between us and the orb but it stayed where it was, just as if it were glued to that spot. Sid was frantic, and speaking more to herself than me.

"What the fuck?! Shit! Motherfucker! Goddammit!" and on it went for about thirty more seconds.

"Sid," I said, trying to get her attention. "Sid. SID. SID! Stop doing that! You're not going to shake that thing!"

"Fuck! How do you know?" she yelled back, still pushing hard on the yoke.

She was about to push her mic button to contact air traffic control, no doubt to let them know what was happening, but I put my hand on her arm.

"Wait, Sid. Wait. I know what that is. Your radio won't work. Just fly normal and breathe. This is about to get weird."

"What the hell? What do you mean you know what this is? What's happening? Did you cause this?" She was sounding scared and pissed off all at the same time

"No, I didn't cause this," I said, trying to keep my voice steady to calm her. "Look, I don't have time to explain what's about to happen, but we shouldn't be harmed in any way, okay?"

"Harmed?! Who the hell would harm us? What are you talking about?" she yelled back.

But that's when the tunnel started to appear. The orb shot ahead and was gone from sight almost instantly. The beautiful view of the mountains ahead of us began to turn foggy as a vortex of haze began to engulf the plane and the view ahead of us. Within seconds, all we could see was a slowly rotating tunnel of clouds ahead of us.

Sid instinctively tried to contact the tower, "Leadville Control! Leadville Control?! Anyone! Mayday! Mayday!" but only the lonely sound of static came back into our headsets. I just looked over at her, waiting for the panic to either pass or spiral out of control. She closed her eyes and I could see her jawline clench. She seemed to be forcing herself to relax and breathe. I wondered if it would work.

Slowly, we could feel the forward motion of the aircraft begin to fade away, and the sounds of the engines started to quiet as we watched the propellers come to a stop. She looked at the left one, then the right one, as they each came to a halt. She seemed to be waiting for the plane to plunge to earth, but it was soon obvious the plane wasn't losing altitude. It simply felt as if we were hanging in the sky. The quietness was deafening. No wind. No engines. No radio or emergency panels. Nothing. I had gone through this once before, many years ago, and I knew what was coming, at least to a point, and I just watched as Sid experienced it for the first time. There was no sense in telling her it was going to be okay because truthfully, I wasn't completely sure myself.

What I did say was, "Sid, listen carefully to me. The plane isn't going to crash but it's not in your control anymore. You can let go of the yoke and relax for a minute." As soon as I said it, I knew what was coming.

"RELAX?!! RELAX?!!!" she screamed at me. "What the fuck is happening?!!! Are you doing this?! Do you KNOW who's doing this?!" All screams.

"No and yes," I said in a steady, low voice. "We have just a few seconds for me to explain, so you can keep yelling at me or I can try and fill you in." Then I just stared at her, waiting for her to decide.

Glaring at me, she said, "Start talking."

8

Baby Steps

*L*earning everything takes some time. To be fair, I didn't learn it all before my first trip to the world. However, I had much more information than a typical soul. Usually, a new soul is introduced to a small-to-medium sized group of other souls in the same stage of development. You would pretty much stay with this group most of eternity, until you either progressed beyond your group, which occasionally happens, or you stop going back to carnate realms. This usually happens when you have reached a level of experience and wisdom and become a guide, teacher or sit on a special council. I'm getting way ahead here but to understand what happened to me next, you have to have a little background so you can see how my progress was so different from other souls.

"Come with me, Timlis," Morah said.
I had never been beyond the nursery at this point and really hadn't thought about somewhere other than here. Morah began to move away from me, so I instinctively followed. Gradually, the blandness of my view changed and suddenly, as if the mist had evaporated, an entire and

overwhelming panorama opened up before me. I could see countless other souls at different distances. Some were next to me and some were just dots in the distance. They were a multitude of different colors. They were beautiful! There were also many different shapes that did not move but were also beautiful. The souls were entering and exiting these shapes. Questions! I had so many questions. I realized I was no longer following Morah when he said, "Timlis, try to keep up with me."

"Who are all of these others? How many are there? What are those shapes? Where are we going?" I blurted out in one long thought.

"All in good time, Timlis, but not here," he said, and I hurried to catch up.

We approached one of the large, beautiful shapes and I stopped. Morah turned to me and waited for me to catch up. Souls were going into and out of a hole in the shape and I was mesmerized. What happened when they entered the shape? I could no longer see them. I wasn't scared, but I was overwhelmed. So much was happening so quickly.

"Please, Morah, tell me what I am seeing," I practically begged.

If a soul could exhale a patient breath, Morah did just that. He came back to my side and stopped.

"The others you see are here to continue their learning, just as you will be doing soon," he began to explain.

"But what are these shapes and why are they going in and out of them," I asked.

"Most of these places are for learning. We use them to separate the different classes and groups from each other when they are attending inside. Right now, the objects look a bit shapeless to you but after you have been to Earth a time or two, the shapes will begin to appear as structures that you associate the type of activity they are known for. What you see and what I see appear differently to each of us, even though they may be the same thing. Timlis, this isn't going to make any sense to you until I give you a briefing and begin teaching you, so please just follow me and this will all begin to make sense to you."

His answers only gave me more questions but before I could protest, he turned and walked/floated into the shape in front of us. I could no longer see him, so I approached the shape and followed. Morah was just inside, facing me. I could tell he was happy and that made me happy. There was another soul standing next to him.

"Timlis, this is Academ. She will be assisting me with your teachings. From this point forward, you are not to speak with anyone else unless we approve it. This is for their protection as much as yours. Do you understand?"

"No. Not really, but I will do what you ask." I really didn't know I even had the possibility to speak with anyone else so not being allowed to do so was of no loss. Everything I did was new and I trusted Morah completely. I had so many questions, I didn't even know which one to ask first. This must have been apparent to Morah.

"We will call today orientation day and give you as much information as we think you can absorb. Relax. Clear your mind and when we have finished we will answer some of your questions. Let's not overdo this all at once. A soul needs time to reflect on new information. Understand?"

"No, Morah, I do not understand but I trust you and will do whatever it is you ask," was my response.

"Then let's begin."

9

Blindsided

I put my finger to my lips to signal her to be quiet and listen, "I have an hour's worth of information to give you and about thirty seconds to get it done. At this moment, the more I tell you, the more trouble you'll be in but I'll give you what you need right now. I'm trying to save the earth. Those are bad aliens. We are in a partial wormhole. In just a few seconds, we'll both be on board their ship. We will probably survive."

As she opened her mouth to ask her first question we were blinded by a light so bright, it seemed to permeate my eyelids and even my fingers as I tried to shield myself from the intensity. I'm really not sure if I screamed or not. I knew this was coming and I still probably yelled. Basic human instinct. It only lasted a few seconds and then the universe went silent and dark. Judging from where I found myself next, I must have been unconscious for some time. I tried to move but I couldn't. I felt as if I were lying on a table and I didn't seem to feel any pain, so I just relaxed for a second and tried to grasp whatever situation I was now in.

I was pretty sure my eyes were open, even though I couldn't see anything, so I let a few minutes pass to see if my eyes adjusted to any light in the room. Nope. Black as ink. I also stretched my hearing to see if I might pick up a conversation in or around wherever I was presently enjoying my vacation. I faintly heard what I hoped was Sid's breathing. It wasn't quite a snore but it wasn't entirely quiet either. After a few more seconds, I tried to get her attention.

"Sid?" I whispered as loudly as I could. I had a feeling that despite the darkness, someone was watching us. It really didn't matter. "SID!" I tried again. This time I got a response, but not a good one. She started screaming like someone falling who couldn't stop themselves.

"Sid! Sid! SID! Easy! I'm here! EASY!" I yelled above her screams.

"I can't get up! Where are we? Why can't I get up?!?" she half-yelled and half-cried. I'm pretty sure that was the same response the first time this had happened to me.

"Sid, listen to me. Listen. I'm just a few feet away and I can't get up either. Listen," I could hear her breathing fast, like a caged animal, which we basically were. "This has happened to me before, so let me give you some information, okay?"

"What the fuck is going on, Jeff?" she yelled at me.

"Like I was telling you before," I tried to sound calm, "I'll tell you plenty when this is over, but for now just be concerned with what I'm able to quickly explain. Once they realize we're awake, I'm sure they won't be far off. They are probably watching us right now"

"THEY?!" she yelled. "You keep saying *they*. Who are *they*, what do *they* want, and where the hell did *they* take us?!"

Okay, I was going to have to give her something here but not enough to get her in trouble. Just enough to calm her down so we might get out of here in one piece.

"Sid, as ridiculous as this sounds, we've been abducted by aliens," I started.

"What the hell, Jeff? You mean we're about to be probed? Are we gonna be sent back to write books about our experience and go to meetings and get made fun of and never work again!?" She was starting to freak out because her voice was getting louder and louder as she went on.

"Sid, look. Chill out and let me try to prepare you for what is probably coming. Some beings will be coming in here in a bit. I can't tell you what they look like because there are different kinds but they may look human or like something from a nightmare. Either way, they took us for a reason and they'll want to find out if we know something or not. After that, they will probably let us go. I don't think they will hurt us. I don't want to scare you but I won't lie to you either. I'm just going by what happened to me the last time this happened to me. I know that's not a lot, but it's the best I can do for now," I said. I knew she had a thousand questions but the less she knew, the less trouble she could get in.

Unfortunately, I had all the answers. I was hoping they didn't realize that, because if they did, they were probably going to hang on to me. For a moment, I wondered where I had gone wrong and how they had tracked me down. I thought I had covered my tracks rather well for the last few years. I usually double- and triple-checked myself but it was obvious that I went left when I should have gone right at some point. I'd have to rethink this when I got out of here. This was going to be a setback for sure but how big of one depended on if I survived this or not. Being dead really slowed me down so I tried to avoid that at all costs.

And then, so gradually that I thought my eyes were playing tricks, the room began to light up. It was as if the walls themselves began to softly glow. Eventually, I could tell we were in a medium-sized room but the walls met the floor in such a way that you couldn't see any edges. It was like one of those photo boxes used to make an object appear as if it's just floating. Finally, there was enough light to see my surroundings.

Sid was to my right, lying on a white, metallic table that appeared to be floating about three feet above the floor. If there was something holding it up, I couldn't see it. I assumed I was lying on a similar table but since I could only move my eyes and not my head, I really had no idea. She still had all of her clothes on so that was a good sign. I didn't feel any weird temperature changes so I was pretty sure all my running gear was just where I left it. Beyond that, I didn't see anything else. The walls and ceiling, what I could see of them, were glowing soft, white light. There were no smells. Nothing. I didn't get any sense of movement so if we were on a ship or vessel, it was very steady.

"This is bullshit!" she said, more to calm herself down than anything. "How fucking long to we have to wait here until the probing begins?! Come on, motherfuckers!"

As if on cue, that's when part of the wall disappeared and two beings walked in. One of them looked very familiar. It was Steve. Dead Steve. Except Steve didn't look especially dead right now. In fact, if I had to put a name to it, Steve looked pissed off. Steve was an alien. Great.

10

School Days

Morah, Academ and I proceeded further into the building and through another hole, which opened into a small room. I call it a room because it had defined areas I could not see beyond, which I was later told were walls. There were also several objects scattered around the room.

"Timlis, this area is called a classroom. It is where you will be taught. Academ and I will meet here with you often and begin to teach and train you for your mission. You are at the very beginning of a very long journey, and we must prepare you for what is to come. The Creator has given us a very special task, and we will do everything within our power to help you achieve your goal. Don't overwhelm yourself with too many questions. Be assured, you will be given more information than any one soul has ever been filled with before you are sent to the world. Let us take the proper time to educate you. There is no hurry here. Only when you leave here is *time* something you will be concerned with."

"What you see around you are call chairs. They have no meaning for you in your current state.

Usually, after a soul has been to the world and has come back, they sometimes like to present themselves in the form that they took while merged with their human. These chairs allow you to sit in one place while we teach you. Later, when you come back to us, you may see and use things differently than you do now. Many of our spaces are recreations of places on the earth, which is where your mission will take place."

"So, clear your mind for a moment while I begin your education. We will give you bits of information and then take a break to let you absorb what you have learned and begin to put it into a larger context. As we progress, the information will begin to make more and more sense to you. You may ask questions but we may not answer them until we believe you have enough knowledge to understand the answer. Do you understand?"

"I believe so," I said. I felt as if everything he just told me was beyond my ability to begin to comprehend. Chair? World? Earth? Time? What did these things mean? I had nothing to compare these words to. I had to trust Morah and Academ to help me. I tried to clear my mind of questions. "I am ready," I said, hoping that I actually was.

"Timlis, I am going to leave you with Academ. She has been teaching souls since before I was as new as you are. She will begin to prepare you and give you an understanding of what you are and who you are. This will be very exciting. I will come back to you later and we will have more discussions." Morah then left as Academ moved to the center and front of the room.

"Timlis, is there anything you want to ask or say before we begin?" she asked.

"I have nothing but questions but they seem so many in number it would be hard to know where to start. I think it best to let you teach and then I will ask questions," I said.

"You are already showing the first spark of wisdom the Creator has imparted upon you," she said. I still didn't know what this meant but I had a feeling I would soon find out.

"Let us begin as close to the start as we can and work our way forward, if there is such a thing," she said. "You and I and everyone in this realm are souls. We were made by the one Creator and we are eternal. Our beginning was imparted upon us by the Creator. Most souls have a single purpose. We are to become as close to perfect as possible, and when that finally occurs, we merge with the Creator again. We do this in two ways."

"First, after we are created and make our way beyond the nursery, we stay in this realm until we have enough knowledge to be sent away for the first time. Creation is a vast and wonderful place and we can decide to be sent nearly anywhere to begin our learning. We experience the universe in as many forms as possible, in as many ways as possible. We find a creature, merge with that being, and together, we benefit. The soul learns as many lessons as can be obtained from that being. Sometimes we are able to do this during just one of their life cycles, if the being is not very complex. Sometimes we visit that same type of being and its world for numerous cycles. The more complex the being, the more we are able to gain and gather more experiences and become more whole."

"The second way we learn is during our time here. We spend time together in classes, learning from those who have mastered a skill. How to build a rock or a plant or a higher life form from which we might one day insert ourselves to learn from. We are the builders of the Creator's universe. The Creator gave us a place to fill and that has been our mission since the beginning. We create whatever is needed to be able to allow every variety of life to be able to exist, grow and flourish. Then we go out into the universe and practice these skills until we master them. "

As Academ spoke, visions appeared that I could only assume represented the things he spoke of. Trying to know what a "rock" was, or a "higher life form" had no meaning to me. I tried to clear my mind and absorb what I was being told and shown. I hoped all of this would eventually make sense to me. It seemed Academ sensed my worries.

"Do not get caught up in what all of this means, Timlis," he said in a very relaxing tone. "You, more than anyone who has come before you, will learn what all of this means. This is just a very large overview. Now, give me some of your questions or concerns."

"What benefits does the other creatures gain from us merging with them?" I asked. It seemed strange for us to need to merge with other beings in order to learn.

"I have an answer that may be more complicated than you ready to understand but I will answer and you may ponder what I tell you. Nearly all creatures that are created have instilled within them very basic instincts. When we first make a being, we create it in such a way as to allow it to develop over a period of time, to allow it to evolve naturally and to adapt to its surroundings while allowing its internal makeup to move toward a better version of itself over many generations. We never make a being in an advanced form. We start with something very basic and let it become its own best version."

"Eventually, sometimes, the being develops into a creature that will be beneficial for us to merge with. We only bind ourselves to beings when we determine it will benefit us as individual souls, and eventually the Creator itself. Not all creatures develop to this point. Not all creatures are used. Many life forms exist that we do not inhabit, and in some rare cases, we are unable to merge with certain seemingly higher life forms. Also, many cease to exist by other circumstances."

"When we are able to and decide to merge with a creature, we give it the ability to develop its mind beyond the basic instincts that it already possesses. We enhance it with the ability to choose more options to better itself. While most beings will focus on just a few of its inherited abilities, we help them see things that they were previously unaware of. In this way, we all achieve a higher greatness."

Again, while Academ spoke, I saw images of what I could only imagine were many of the different beings that we merge with throughout the realm of creation. They came in every shape and size and color, well beyond my meager comprehension. I simply trusted that what I was seeing was real and assigned no value to it, beyond just acceptance of what I was being told.

"You have said that I am different from other souls. You have said souls are put in classes together. Why am I different and what is this mission that you spoke of?" I asked, not sure if I was ready for the answers.

"Timlis, we have never changed the outcome of a being's development once we set it in motion. Once we have created it, the being either adapts to its surroundings and advances, or it ceases to exist. This has been going on since the very beginning of creation."

"We were able to create a being, not long ago, that was far superior to any we had ever created previously. Most beings we merge with are able to teach and advance our souls in a few different ways and then we move on to a different being, somewhere else in the realm of the universe."

"However, this one particular creation far outshined any other in its development. Even though it was very early in its stages of advancement, we were able to merge and learn more from it than any other. In fact, a soul could enter one of these beings, and once its cycle ended, enter another one, and then another and another. Each time, learning more, and more and more. The possibilities seemed nearly endless in the different degrees of lessons that could be gained from this one creature. The Creator himself even took note of this particular planet and its unique life form."

"Then a problem took hold. Other creatures from different worlds also found this planet. One specific race of beings became a problem for us. They began using the planet for its resources and its beings for their own benefit. They had done this before many times over on other worlds and, until now, it was never an issue. However, this time was different. As they began to blend themselves with the planet's inhabitants, we were no longer able to merge into them. It was never their intention to change them in this way, but the offspring of these mergers produce a being that we can no longer become part of. If left unchecked, they may destroy the race completely, and we will lose a valuable asset to the Creator. We do not wish to lose such a unique being from whom we learn so much," she said.

"Your mission will be to drive out the invading beings and allow the original inhabitants to continue to grow and develop. We believe they have the potential to be the most substantial creation to exist one day, if we can only stop the other beings from influencing them."

"Timlis, to lose the ability to merge with these creatures would be a great loss to our purpose. The Creator himself agreed to allow an obtrusion, which has never happened. It was decided that something must be done. Then you were created."

11

Shit Meets Fan

Life would get boring if absolutely everything went according to plan. Today was not going to be boring. Steve, the alien, had obviously been on Earth a long time, at least long enough to perfect the smirk that was presently spread across his stupid face. Why couldn't Steve just stay dead? Judging from the lack of a large hole in his head, he was obviously a "lizard alien" who had made friends with the "greys". Lizards didn't have the kind of tech needed to fix head holes, but greys did. Too bad.

"Hey, Steve," I said, "you're looking fit and trim today."

He walked over to the table I laid on, grabbed my arm, spinning my road ID around to look at the name I had etched into it. "Hello, Jim, or Jeff, or Time Baron, or whatever you're calling yourself today," he said in his best American dialect of English he could muster, with just the proper hint of disdain. "I think we have some unfinished business to discuss. Would you like to start or should I just begin our famous, traditional alien probing?"

"Steve, you forked tongue piece of shit! If I see one little probe, or laser, or anything that doesn't look like a cheeseburger while I'm stuck in this tin can of a flying garbage truck, I'll make sure the next fifteen bullets don't miss a single heart in that slimy body. You may look like a human but we all know you are just wearing your favorite costume so you don't look like a nightmare that escaped from a zoo," I said in a calm tone with an equally snide smirk on my face.

Apparently, Steve isn't the kind of lizard who takes criticism well, since he reached out and slapped me across the face so fast that I barely had time to shut my eyes. Yowza, that stung! But I opened my eyes and just smiled.

"Steve, Steve, Steve. Is that move in the lizard handbook of how to extract information from an Earth abductee? You suck as an interrogator. Why don't you ask your grey buddy how this works?" I said as I felt the heat from his slap on my face.

He just stared at me and I stared back at him. Then he got that fucked up stupid smile on his face again and I instantly knew what was next. He took two steps back and motioned with his left hand towards Sid. She had watched our exchange out of the corner of her eye, saying nothing. That was about to change.

"I think this will go much faster if we start with your friend," he said, "and just come back to you later. We've all seen enough Earth movies to know you will give up the information I want if I start slicing off pieces of your friend. Maybe she will only lose a few toes or fingers before you decide to tell us what we want. Hopefully, it won't come to a leg or arm. And just to let you know that I'm a man of my word, I'll take one finger just for laughs. You like to laugh don't you, Jeff?" Steve said.

"Lizard dick, if you touch one hair on her head, this entire crew won't make it out of here alive," I promised.

"Lizard dick? Is that how we're going to play this, Jeff? Fine. Remove the left foot!" he yelled to no one in particular.

Before Sid or I could protest, a beam of light came from the ceiling and judging from the scream, sliced off Sid's foot, just as ordered.

"Ahhhhhhhhhhhhhhhhhhhhhhh!" she screamed, "Motherfucker! Ahhhhhhhhhhhhhhhhhhh!" then she took a few deep breaths and passed out.

"Okay, Jeff, when she wakes up, we will take off a little more. Want to tell me where the ship is or do I keep removing more pieces of your friend?"

I closed my eyes and took a few deep breaths. Calm. Be Calm. I had been in far more serious situations than this and letting my emotions take over did not improve my odds of surviving. I had too much work to do here, and dying would really hamper this operation. I refused to let this idiot kill me, and hopefully, I could save Sid, too.

All this time, the "grey" who entered the room with Steve had done nothing. It just stood there, watching the exchange. It showed no evidence of being happy, sad, or annoyed when Sid's blood went squirting all over the spotless white room. The greys were cold and calculating. There would be no bargaining with them without some leverage. At the moment, I had none. However, the lizards seemed to be about as flawed as humans, maybe more. They had just been around much longer, so they were much better at manipulating people. So much so that they had infiltrated every single facet of human government, religion and business. With the greys help, they had taken over the entire Earth for their own purposes. Humankind was presently fucked, but I knew how to unfuck it and I was very close to making that happen. However, being on this table was not on my agenda for making this happen very soon so I had to change my situation, pronto.

My advantage over lizard Steve was he still thought he was dealing with a normal human. Technically, I was a normal human, just one who had several lifetimes of information within him to draw upon. I had studied countless types of aliens, and especially the ones that presently inhabited Earth and posed the largest threat to humankind. I just had to use that knowledge to get myself and Sid out of this little distraction.

"Steve, I'll tell you what. Let me off this table and you and I can have a little fun. If you beat me, then you can stop spilling blood all over your pretty white room and I'll tell you everything I know," I said.

"That is an incredibly stupid idea, Baron. First, if you knew anything about us, you would know we are far stronger and superior to humans in every way. There is no way you could possibly win. Second, why should I even begin to give you that opportunity? All I have to do is keep slicing up your friend and you'll talk. You humans always do."

"Maybe," I said, "but maybe not. You might kill my friend then kill me. Then where would you be? I bet your boss will be pissed off if you killed me and didn't find out where the ship is."

I knew the mention of the ship would get his attention. I also knew that Steve was not the guy in charge of this mission. He would be reporting to his superior and failure would not be tolerated, especially when he was this close to his prize. He felt he was within reach of getting the information and that would make him sloppy, at least I hoped so. Lizards were extremely prideful and believed themselves so superior over humans that I hoped this would make him drop his guard and act out of instinct.

He did not answer immediately so I knew he was thinking it over. He looked back at Sid, still unconscious. He walked closer to Sid and stood by her side. He looked down at her and then back at me.

"Here's the deal," he said. "When I win, you will tell me everything I want to know. If I feel you have hidden nothing from me, I will wipe both of your memories and put you back where I found you. If I feel you are being less than completely truthful, I will slice up your friend while you watch, then keep you a prisoner for as long as I can keep you alive, which can be a very long time."

I knew Steve's promise was hollow. If he ever learned where the ship was, he would kill both of us.

"Deal," I said.

12

Mission Notes

I left class and let the information swirl around inside of me. I had so many questions and felt anxious to learn more. Academ assured me that we would continue our classes until I was sufficiently ready to begin my mission. I could certainly feel the importance of what was being placed upon me but because I had never experienced merging with another being, or what that actually felt like, some of this was lost on me. I felt fine just as I was. What possible lessons could be learned merging with others that I could not learn here? So much to discover. So much to experience.

I met Academ again for another lesson. I think she could feel the changes within me. I certainly didn't feel like the same soul who had left the nursery only a short time ago. Is this how it felt after merging with another being?

"Okay, Timlis," she said, "give me your thoughts and questions."

"Who are these other creatures who also inhabit this world that are causing the problem?" I asked.

"They are creatures that were formed well before this planet even existed. They eventually progressed until they were able to leave their own planet and explore the cosmos. We do not have the ability to merge with them. Therefore, they succumb to their most basic instincts, one of which is to dominate other worlds. "

"Is this a common instinct among creatures or just this one?" I asked.

"This is a common trait you will find in nearly every creature created," he explained. "If a being progresses enough to survive and thrive, it has done so because it has the self-preservation quality within it. Initially, this is a welcome attribute. However, if left unchecked, this quality can overpower the being and can eventually become its dominant characteristic. If we are able to merge with the being, we are able to tamp down this urge to an acceptable degree that allows it to continue its progress but without overwhelming it."

"Until recently, there has not been a problem with this or with other beings like this," he continued. "If these creatures took over a planet and its beings, the loss to us was so minimal we barely took notice. We simply had too many other options available to let this concern us."

"So, the beings on this planet are the best matches for souls to learn from?" I asked.

"We believe so," he stated. "There are countless beings scattered throughout creation. Some have advanced in many ways. Some have left their home planets to travel the cosmos. Some have barely advanced since they were created. Most have been beings we have been able to merge with and learn from. Some have not. All have different qualities which lend to our goal to learn and experience all that there is."

"What will my mission be?" I asked.

"You will go to this planet, merge with a being, and begin to learn, experience, and plan," he said.

"How will this be different from any other soul who is sent there?" I asked.

"All other souls lose the ability to remember their previous trips to a world. They are also unable to remember being in this realm. However, each time we send you there, you will have the full knowledge of all that has happened from the previous trips, as well as what you learn here. You will use your knowledge and experiences from being carnate and here to your advantage. You must first learn how to be a human being and eventually discover how to rid the planet of the creatures that endanger the humans," she explained.

"Why are other souls not allowed to remember their previous trips to this world?" I asked. It seemed this would only help a soul if they remembered each time they merged.

"When a soul returns to this realm, they remember all previous carnations, whether it is to this world, or any other. They use this culmination of knowledge and experiences to decide what they need to learn and experience the next time they merge. They are then able to plan this next trip, along with the help of teachers and other wise souls."

"But if a soul would return to a different being with full knowledge of previous trips, they would not be able to focus on their goals because they would be overwhelmed with all of their previous experiences. This would stop them from further growth, which would undermine our existence," she said.

"Will I not be overwhelmed by all of my previous trips and experiences if I continue to remember my past carnations?" I asked.

"Timlis, I'm not going to tell you that it may not have some effect upon you. We have never tried this with a soul before so the outcome is unknown. We have taken some extra precautions, however. First, the creator himself created you differently than any previous soul. Your ability to possess and use this great amount of information will be your greatest asset. Next, when other souls leave this realm to merge with a being, they leave a significant degree of themselves here. While part of the soul is learning from its being, the other part remains here and continues to absorb lessons. When the merged being eventually ceases, the soul is released to return here and the soul reunites as a whole and its knowledge is shared."

"This, also, is where you will be different. Sometimes the beings that we merge with are able to somewhat dominate the soul. This is because a specific being can be unusually strong-willed and the soul will not take enough of itself into the being to dominate its decisions. You, however, cannot be left to chance. You will take nearly all of your soul into the being you merge with, leaving only the smallest trace behind. This trace will not learn or experience lessons while the majority is away. It will simply exist to wait for the majority to return," she said.

"Why am I to be alone in this cause? Why has the creator not made others like me to help us with this mission?" I asked.

"We cannot risk the invading creatures becoming aware of your mission. At this time, they are not merging with and destroying this population in a manner that will end them in the foreseeable future. However, they have done this on enough previous planets that we believe they will eventually take over and extinguish this entire population. If they learn of you and your assignment, they may speed up their efforts before you are able to drive them out. If we make others like you, the possibility of them discovering our pursuit could be uncovered, and our efforts thwarted."

"When do we begin?" was all I had left to ask.

"Soon," she said.

13

Plan B

I'm a planner. I wasn't always, but I learned quickly through necessity. If you don't have a goal, then you can't plot a path to arrive at your destination. I had a mission, and a plan to accomplish that mission. But I never have just one plan because it's a rare day that Plan A ever works out. Why even make a Plan A then? Because you can't make Plan B without Plan A. It rarely ever stops there though. Sometimes I go as far as Plan G, because a few times, Plans A-F have gone out the window. The day it went THAT wrong, I had to make shit up on the fly and while I don't have any problems with improvising, it's not the best way to ensure a successful outcome. I've failed enough times to know better now, hence, Plan F and G.

So when I left my rented flat in Leadville to go for a run and lure Steve to a secluded area to remove him, I didn't depend on that entirely to work. Hope does not ensure victory. Which brings me to being incapacitated on a table in an alien spaceship, with a previously dead, human-looking lizard staring down at me. Thank goodness I had studied these idiots long enough to know how to push the right buttons to manipulate them. Sometimes. But today looked like my day.

Many lifetimes ago, or should I say between lifetimes, I visited the greys as a soul to learn about them and their technology. If they were part of the problem, I needed to know what motivated them as well as their advanced technology. As a soul, that was not a concern, but as a human, it might save me in several different ways. Today was one of those days.

Lizard Steve backed up a few steps and nodded to Mr. Grey and a second later I could feel the invisible restraints removed. Steve must have thought I'd take a second to collect myself before engaging. Wrong. I didn't give Steve even half a second to prepare himself. I pulled off my road ID as I swung my legs to the side, pushed the hidden button on the side, and swept the laser beam across the room, slicing the walls, the grey, and Steve. The beam only had enough power to be good for a few seconds but it was enough. The grey and Steve were lying on the floor, the smell from slicing through both of them hung heavy in the air. There was very little blood since the beam instantly cauterized their wounds but that also meant that both of them were still somewhat alive.

"You motherfucker!" Steve spat at me in his best Earth English. "I'm going to *gurgle, gurgle, gurgle*," he said.

"What's that Steve, old buddy?" I said matter-of-factly. "I didn't catch that last part. Seems that your blood is coming out of your mouth. Sorry, I can't stick around for the rest of this conversation; we've got places to go." At that, I kicked lizard Steve hard in the head and his eyes promptly closed.

The grey was doing a bit worse. The top half was pulling itself along with its hands trying to reach its bottom half. I'm not sure why, I didn't have time to investigate. These bastards communicate telepathically and since I didn't know how big this ship was or how many buddies he had outside the door, I had to act quickly.

I knelt down beside Mr. Grey and gave him some options. I pointed my modified Road ID at his face and said, "You have three seconds to release my friend from that table and open that door or you get one more slice down the middle of your head. 3. 2…," at which time the door slid open. He didn't need to know my weapon was out of laser power. I grabbed the lower half of Steve and threw it across the threshold, just in case the door decided to try to close again. Steve wouldn't mind. I then gave Mr. Grey a quick whack on the head to make sure he was less than conscious.

It was time to get off this roller coaster but first I had to help Sid. I grabbed her arms and pulled her up and into a sitting position. I then maneuvered her so I could hoist her over my shoulder into a fireman carry. Her boot with her foot was still lying on the table. It seemed strange to leave it there so I grabbed it as well. If this rust bucket of a space ship was even a moderately supplied recon vehicle, it would have a sickbay. Somehow, Steve had gotten himself patched up from his encounter with me so maybe this is where he received his medical treatment.

As soon as I exited, there was a wall in front of me and a hall that went to the left and right that slightly curved in either direction so I couldn't see very far either way. There was no way to know which way to go, and worse, no way to tell if there was anyone else on this thing. No sense in worrying about stuff you can't control and I was in too much of a hurry to ponder so I went left and moved as quickly as possible. I'd only scouted one ship in the past and I'm sure they must have changed things since then. But a door is a door and a ship is a ship, so hopefully, I could still recognize enough to get us out of here.

I was beginning to lose some hope when I went thirty feet or so and couldn't find a single door. I knew they were probably in the wall but I didn't have the capacity to open one. That's when Mr. Grey #2 started to walk out of the door that just appeared eight feet in front of me on the left wall. If a grey's eyes could possibly get any larger than they already are, this one made it happen. He apparently had no idea I was coming down the hall and when he saw me with Sid over my shoulders, practically sprinting at him, he was startled to the point of momentary indecision, which was all of the time I needed.

Thank goodness Sid was still unconscious, because I took two more fast steps and launched myself and Sid right at Mr. Grey #2, upon which we all hit the floor, with me on top of Grey. I did a pretty good job of keeping Sid from bouncing around too much but I think I broke some pieces inside Grey. He actually let out a little gaspy sound from his slit of a mouth and his stare was a bit blank so he was somewhat dazed.

The lizards are the greys' muscle, so in a one-on-one situation, a grey is rarely a physical challenge to a human. However, the little bastards have the power of mind control over most humans which makes them dangerous and a pain in the ass. Thankfully, the Creator saw fit to make me immune from this parlor trick and I've been grateful ever since.

Before he (I never figured a way to tell the difference) could completely gain his senses, I put my hands around his throat and spoke very evenly and softly, "Hello, my friend." I waited for him to try his mind control on me to let him understand it wouldn't work. "If you summon more friends, I will rip your head from you neck before they get ten feet away from me. Nod your head if you understand."

I knew these creatures had been on Earth long enough to understand every language perfectly. I gave his tiny neck a squeeze and he nodded his head as his eyes closed slightly at the register of pain.

"First, tell me, are there more of you on this ship?" I asked.

His head bobbed towards me once.

"I don't care what you tell them but you need to make sure they stay away from us and don't know we are presently free. Can you make that happen?" I asked again.

His head once again bobbed. I didn't know if I was being outwitted or was actually pulling this off but either way, I was serious about removing his big head so maybe he understood my willingness to carry out my promises.

"I need two things from you. First, you are going to take me to your medical room. I'm about to let you off the floor but will be pointing my weapon at you. Your buddy down the hall is now in two separate pieces. If you make a gesture I decide is against my friend and me, you will also be in more pieces than you presently are. Understand?" I threatened.

He looked me in the eyes and nodded. These guys showed zero emotions, which made conversations and threats hard to pull off. Was this guy going for my bluff or was I about to get my ass handed to me by 300 approaching grey, naked Keebler elves sans cookies? I had a feeling I'd find out very quickly. I slowly let him off the ground, all the while pointing my spent Road ID weapon at him which, truthfully, felt a little silly.

He wasted no time and began walking down the hall as I hoisted Sid back over my shoulders. After about forty more feet (this ship was pretty good sized) a door opened on our left and he stepped in. I resisted the urge to stop and check the interior before stepping in since I felt I was screwed if this was a trick. I just took a few steps inside and the door closed behind me.

The inside looked much like the room we had been held in except it was entirely empty. No tables. Nothing. These guys weren't much for adding homey touches to the décor.

"I want you to put my friend's foot back where it belongs and make it as good as new," I said, without giving him the option to deny it could be done. I figured if they could bring Steve back from the dead, they could easily put a foot back on a leg. But how long did something like this take. Ten seconds? Ten days? I felt like we were pushing our luck with every passing second. A table instantly emerged from the floor. Several other devices emerged from the walls and ceiling. The grey looked at me, then looked at the table which I took as "put her on the table". Did I just understand what he wanted me to do or did I hear that in my head? Either way, I gently laid Sid down on the table. Sheepishly, I grabbed her foot from my jacket and placed it on the table next to her leg, wondering how this worked.

The grey walked over to the table and picked up the severed foot. He turned it over slowly, as if studying it. He then held it higher and a robotic arm type of device descended from the ceiling, grasped the booted foot, and then disappeared back into the ceiling. The sides of the table appeared to clamshell close, enveloping Sid completely. I had no idea if they were repairing her or disintegrating her. The grey walked over to the table and rested its hand against the edges of the enclosure over Sid. Was he telling it what to do or was this just some gesture?

What must have been ten, long minutes dripped by and the grey took two steps backward, away from the table, as the clamshell slid away and back into the sides of the table. Sid was still lying on the table so at least her atoms weren't obliterated. I try to see the glass half-full. What was immediately noticeable was she was completely naked. However, from what I could see, she now possessed two feet again. I took a step closer to see how the foot looked, at which time her eyes fluttered and she almost instantly woke up.

The last thing she remembered before passing out was the blinding pain associated with losing a foot so she wasn't exactly giggly when she woke up.

"Hey!" she yelled, as her eyes darted back and forth while sitting up. It was a strange combination of reactions on her face as she looked down and noticed she was naked but at the same instant realized she once again had two feet. I couldn't begin to imagine what was going on in her head.

"What the hell is going on?" she yelled again. "Why am I naked? How did I get my foot back?" then she looked at me and at the grey, then back at me. "Jeff, what the hell happened?!"

"Can I tell you later after we find you some clothes and get the hell out of here?" I said.

She looked at us both again. "Fuck, Jeff, you keep saying you'll ell me stuff later but we never seem to get there. Fine. "

I looked back at Mr. Grey and said, "Clothes?" as I tugged at my own jacket, hoping to give him a hint.

Then that same arm that took her foot into the ceiling reappeared with what seemed to be her flight suit but this one was mended, or cleaned, or recreated, since it didn't have the rips and blood from the previous jumpsuit. Then a small, translucent bag came down and was held in front of her. Sid must have been pretty comfortable in her own skin because she wasn't really making attempts to cover herself up in any way. She stared at the bag, then at the grey and back at the bag. She slowly reached out and as she pulled on the bag, the arm let it go and ascended back into the ceiling.

The top to the bag was open and she peered inside. She half-smiled and half-smirked so that was a good reaction.

"It's my underwear and my boots," she said. She dumped the contents onto the table and then just gave me a blank stare.

I stared back, waiting for her to get dressed so we could get moving. Nothing. Just a stare.

"Uh, do you mind turning around so I can get dressed?" she said.

"Are you serious? I don't think I can see much more than I've already seen," I said, but I just got *the look.* Women. I will never figure them out and I've even been one before.

I walked over to the grey and stood next to him then motioned for him to spin around with me so we were both facing the wall. Maybe we were communicating telepathically or maybe he was just good at charades but we both spun at the same time and faced the wall. I think I even heard him give a sigh of "you've gotta be kidding me" or maybe that was me. After a couple of minutes and some shuffling sounds, we heard, "Okay, let's get the fuck out of here."

"Wait!" she said, "where the hell is my jacket?"

"Really, you're worried about a jacket?" I began to protest.

"Either that jacket magically appears or your friend is getting this new boot up his ass or whatever other orifice I can find to cram it into!" she said rather harshly.

I just looked at Mr. Grey, seeing if he understood what she said and the gravity with which it was intoned.

Suddenly, the handy, dandy ceiling arm appeared and gently handed the leather jacket back to Sid. "Okay. *Now* we can go," she said.

"Okay, my earless pal, time for you to get us home." He looked thrilled.

14

INTEL

(Author's Note: I'll be using words like "planet" and "stars" and other descriptive English words. These are not the actual words that came across during conversations. They are just the easiest way to tell the story in a manner that can be understood by the reader. Don't get hung up on these things.)

"Timlis, today we are going to go on a travel mission. You will need to know about the beings who are trying to undermine our objectives," Morah said.

I had gone into my normal classroom, expecting to see Academ, but found Morah instead. I had not spent much time with Morah since Academ had been instructing me so I was happy to spend this time with him. I had no reference for what *travel* meant but anything new was a joy to encounter. I waited to see what this could mean.

"Do you have any questions, Timlis?" he asked.

"I always have questions, Morah, but I will wait until you take me on this mission to form better ones."

I think I registered some happiness from him with this answer.

"We are going to travel to the home planet of a race of beings who call themselves Dracons. In their own world, they look like a larger version of a creature found on the planet we are trying to save from them. You will see for yourself. We do not merge with these beings so while they are advanced, they are driven by greed and pleasure and most of that is derived from taking over and ruling other planets," he said.

"Come close to me, Timlis, and I shall take us to Dracon," he said.

As I came next to Morah, our lights began to merge at the edges and with that, we were no longer in the room at the school. We seemed to be in a swirl of light and although I felt nothing different, I had a sense we were moving great distances very quickly. It was an interesting trip and since it was my first, I felt what I later would describe as excitement. Each new emotion was a unique experience and Academ had told me to expect different feelings inside of me as our teachings progressed. I didn't fully understand what she meant by that statement then, but I learned it since, and was experiencing a new one now. I liked excitement.

When the colors slowed down and seem to melt away, we were in a dark place with tiny lights surrounding us. However, the overwhelming object in front of us was an enormous disc with various shapes and colors inside of it.

"Tell me what this is Morah," I begged. I had never seen anything like this at the school or my chamber.

"This object is called a planet and this one's name is Dracon. It is the home of the Draconians, the race we will learn more about during this class. We are some distance away right now so we can see the cosmos nearest the planet and the entire planet itself. Now we will slowly approach the planet, so you get accustomed to the shapes and sizes as they relate to themselves and other things on it and near it," he instructed.

With that, we came closer to the planet. I noticed it moved so that new views were coming into my view, which made me realize that this object was not a disc, but was round on all sides.

"Tell me what I am seeing, Morah," I asked. It all looked beautiful. What could it all be?

"Most planets with life forms we use to merge with are much like this one. They vary in different ways but for the most part, they share more than they don't. For instance, this one is larger than the one for your mission. The blue parts are water (usually when he describes a thing like *blue* to me he shows an image to me that represents the idea or object he wants me to learn about). Most of the other parts are land and this is where the Dracons live. The white misty parts that seem to move are clouds, which float above the land. Once you are carnate upon the Earth, you will learn more about these things for yourself. Our main lesson here today is to learn about the Draconians themselves," he explained.

This was a bit overwhelming. I felt as if I had gone from a very small place to one so vast I just couldn't comprehend it. So much new information and new questions were exploding within me, I didn't know where to begin. Morah sensed this immediately and we stopped for a moment.

"Timlis, be easy. Clear yourself of questions and information for a moment and just stop to enjoy what you are experiencing around you. Look at the tiny specks of light and their many colors. Look at the planet as it turns before us. See the sun of the planet and its glorious beauty. This was all made possible by the Creator. I have been made so long, I sometimes forget to stop and enjoy this divine wonder."

I did as he said and allowed the vastness of what was before me soak into my core. What lay before me was infinite. The ability to comprehend it all was well beyond my meager abilities, at least right now, but that was fine. Right now, all I needed to do was look. This would always be one of the best days of my existence. The weight of the universe was not upon my shoulders yet, but that was all about to change. I soaked up the last few bits of joy from this moment. It was time to learn.

"I feel I am ready now," I said.

We once again began to slowly descend towards the planet until I could no longer see the cosmos, just the planet itself. We pierced the clouds and came closer and closer to one of the large pieces of land. Soon, I could make out objects on the land which reminded me of the buildings at home that housed my classroom and other places the souls used to gather. How strange it seemed.

"Timlis, the Draconians will not be able to see or perceive us in any way. They will not try to interact with us, so we are able to watch and learn about them," he said.

"Why is that?" I asked.

"Until we merge with another being, we hold no form that most carnates may sense," he said.

"Most?" I asked.

"Of those beings in which we are able to merge, some of the souls within are advanced to the degree that they allow their being to comprehend the world beyond the physical they inhabit. Some are able to speak to us in soul form, and some are even able to see our light. It is a rare thing, but it happens on occasion. The Draconians do not have such abilities, since no soul has merged with them."

We came to the level where we were among the Draconians and their structures. They moved in curious ways, not the graceful ways in which a soul is able. Their bodies were covered with various degrees of green. They further covered themselves with other colors. Some used their own bodies to move about between the structures, some were inside small structures that moved about on the ground, while others seemed to be inside of objects that moved among the clouds. It was all very interesting to watch. There seemed to be a purpose to everyone's movement.

At home, you could immediately feel how another soul felt, even from a distance. Their colors changed and they radiated vibrations that announced sentiment. Although I did not have close contact with many souls, I could still detect these things. But here, these beings gave off no feelings that I could describe.

"What is your impression Timlis?" Morah asked.

"I feel nothing from these beings. Do they not have feelings?" I asked.

"Yes, Timlis, they feel a great many things and that is one of the lessons you are here to learn. They do not easily extend their emotions outwardly. Not only to us, but even between each other. It is a sign of weakness others among their society would take advantage of. The better they are able to hide these feelings, the higher they are regarded among their own kind. However, their

overwhelming characteristics are fear, hate, and the desire to dominate over each other and anyone else, whether it be here or abroad. It is their subtle ways of showing these traits that you must learn to recognize," he explained.
I had much to learn.

15

Leaving Oz

The greys and the lizards, officially the Draconians, have entirely separate reasons for being on Earth but that doesn't stop them from occasionally working together when they find a common benefit. Today's operation was clearly being run by the lizards. Steve had a mission and he apparently requisitioned a team of greys to help him. The greys were masters when it came to snatching, also known as abducting, beings. They had the technology to get in, grab, and get out, usually without anyone ever knowing. Usually. Recently, humans had progressed to the point that not only did they realize there were alien beings around them but they were being taken away and periodically returned.

It was the return part I was most interested in. The last time this happened to me, I was at a clear disadvantage. Being a newbie abductee I didn't have as much intel on the inner workings of the actual process of moving creatures to and from their crafts as I might have wanted to. I never imagined that I might be the one taken one day. However, since that first trip, many years ago, I decided to investigate the process, just in case I needed it one day. Today was "one day." Now came the tricky part. I had to convince Mr. Grey to send us back from whence we came. I had no idea if this particular grey was the commander of this ship, the doctor, or the guy who pushed the mop. I suppose, in the end, it didn't really matter. He was who I had to work with so I'd just do my best. I'd been around greys enough to know that this particular one didn't seem to have a dog in the hunt of this operation, so hopefully, we could come to some arrangement.

"Okay, here's what we're going to do," I said to my short, color-lacking friend. I knew he understood what I was saying, either through the actual words, or a telepathic link. I had the ability to shield my thoughts from our alien friends and also the ability to let them read me when it was convenient for both of us. Right now, I was letting it all hang out. Read away buddy.

"You are going to lead us to the transport room (I hoped that translated correctly; I'm sure they had an official name for the room but since I hadn't seen any signs on the doors, I was just making this up as I went) and put us back where we came from."

He didn't look overly interested in what I was saying so I decided to give him some motivation.

"Take a look at the room you were holding us in and I think you'll agree that I came prepared to take some actions you may find disagreeable if my demands are not met," I said, with a stern look on my face. At least I hoped he understood it to be stern. Who knew?

At once, three screens appeared suspended in mid-air. They weren't really screens, as they had no actual structure to them. It was more as if a mist or different kind of air appeared before us that allowed the scene from the room to play in front of us. You've got to love these guys and their tech. In the end, that's really what my mission was all about but we'll get to that later.

On the screens before us, different views of our previous room appeared. There were four pieces of the two captors on the floor, each sliced neatly across their mid-sections. Surprisingly, one of them, Steve, still appeared to be alive. I had kicked lower-half Steve back into the room after our hasty getaway. That guy has nine lives, or however many a lizard's cat has. Either way, he wasn't dead. Yet. I was hoping this would make some impression upon my present color challenged buddy. I pointed my Road ID at his big head.

"Unless you would like to be disassembled like those guys, I suggest you fire up the transporter and beam us back down, Scotty," I said. Man, I hoped he knew that reference, because it was awesome! I looked over at Sid and she actually rolled her eyes at me. Come on! It's never a bad time for a Star Trek call back. This was a tough crowd.

He looked at me for a moment and started out the door. These doors didn't actually open or slide sideways with a cool *whoosh* sound, they more or less just misted away as you approached them and then became part of the wall again after you passed through. It was as if they knew your intention to enter or leave and didn't do that trick if you just happened to be walking by. I could use doors like that at my houses on Earth.

We turned left out of the door and continued further down the hall.

"Also," I mentioned to His Greyness, "steer clear of any of your friends. Kapish?" Let's see if he understood that little Italian nugget.

He turned his head sideways and just looked at me. Did I detect an alien eye roll? Impossible. They had no whites to their eyes but just the same, it seemed like an eye roll to me. Sid was just nodding her head back and forth. I don't think she believed I was taking this very seriously. I guess I can see her point of view. She had just been whisked away from her airplane in mid-flight, held down on a table, had her foot sliced off, and now found herself on an alien spacecraft. I suppose I could try to seem more concerned, for appearances. We stopped and once again, a door on our left opened. It looked the same as the other rooms. Off white floor, walls and ceiling.

Bare. These guys might abduct an interior decorator next time. Would a picture of Mrs. Grey and the grey kids back home be so terrible to hang on a wall?

The three of us stepped inside and the door reformed into a wall. In my mind I added the *whoosh* sound effect. Then Mr. Grey just stopped and stared at us with his big, ink-black eyes. That never stops being creepy. They are a hard bunch to read, body language-wise. Was he planning our demise or remembering he forgot to take the laundry out of the dryer? He apparently decided we were clueless as he lifted his long skinny arm and pointed to the far wall.

Sid and I exchanged looks and both walked to the opposite wall. Hopefully a giant laser beam didn't appear from the ceiling and separate our atoms. I was placing way too much trust in the assumption that our new friend would allow us to leave. Maybe he understood that the sooner we left, the sooner he could try to reassemble his buddies back in the "abduction room". Who knew what motivated this guy.

As we reached the wall and turned to look back at the grey, a control panel emerged and formed from the floor, just in front of him. No words were spoken, and no "see ya later" wave as he passed his hand over the panel and the room misted slowly away from our view.

I have no idea if we were unconscious for a split second or three months but we both woke up at the same time, back in the seats of the aircraft we had been plucked from. The plane itself didn't appear to be moving and as we looked out of the front window, the swirling vortex of clouds in front of us began to fade away, allowing sunlight to pour into the cockpit. I felt the heat of the sun on my face and almost felt safe again. All good signs. Except for one little detail. The engines were still off.

I think we both realized the problem at the exact same millisecond. For a moment, the universe was quiet. Not a single sound. Being several thousand feet in the air in an airplane, above some mountains, you want there to be some sound. The sound of engines to be exact. The quiet was deafening.

We both looked at each other and said, "Oh, shit!" The plane had no forward motion. No lift. Nada. We were a rock in the air and this rock only had one direction to travel. Down.

"Get the engines going and I'll try to keep us under some kind of control," I said as calmly as I could muster. Having Sid freak out right now wasn't going to get either one of us out of this situation. I knew she had the best knowledge of this aircraft so she would get the job done much faster than I would fumbling around trying to re-educate myself with this model as we plummeted towards the earth. I could certainly hold my own with the stick and pedals as she worked her magic.

"You didn't mention you knew how to fly earlier," she half-yelled and half-sneered at me as her hands deftly began hitting switches as she looked to her left and right, hoping to see some rewards to her efforts.

I, on the other hand, wasn't having much luck. We needed enough speed for either the flaps or rudder to have any effect on the stability of this plane. Right now we were just heading mostly nose first towards the beautiful snow-capped mountains below us. We had less than sixty seconds before this plane would make an ugly spot on Williams Mountain.

The g-forces from the fall were making this an interesting challenge. The fall was good and bad and it would be a contest to see which won out in the end. The bad part was the faster we moved towards the mountain, the sooner we would hit it. The good part was, the faster we moved towards the mountain, the better our airspeed and the more control I was able to have over the plane. Sticky wicket, as our British friends enjoy saying. All the while, Sid was doing her best to get the engines talking.

"Why aren't you starting?" she yelled at the plane. "Come on! Come on! Come on!"

Just as I started to get a hint of control, I realized it wouldn't be enough in time. At best, I'd just make a more graceful crash than nosing directly in. I prepared myself for what was coming next and then I heard the sound. The engine on the right came to life and Sid pushed it to full throttle as a second later, the left one sputtered up. Sid punched it to full throttle as well and now we were going even faster towards the mountain but it was exactly what we needed. We both pulled back on the stick and instinctively steered for the pass between the mountains peaks. I'd be lying if I didn't admit to asking my friends above for a little help.

We were both screaming out loud as the plane pulled out of the dive and began to level out, and then climb again. Between the screaming engines and the speed from the fall, we had full control over the plane, but that didn't mean we were going to clear the pass in front of us. There was no turning left or right, as that would just plow us into a rock wall faster. It was either clear the pass or not.

It was so close. I really thought we might pull it off since luck had been so good to us for the last hour. The treetops were just starting to scratch the belly of the plane when the propellers began slicing off some pine needles.

"Shit," was all I got out. From the corner of my eye, I could see Sid giving it all she had, but she still had that look on her face that told me she knew what was about to happen.

It was everything you could imagine and more. Little explosions lit fires for a moment as both wings were torn from the fuselage. The entire plane, or what was left of it, began shaking violently. The stick just became something to hold onto and brace against as the nose plowed through the heavily scented pine trees. We were now passengers in an ongoing wreck. There were sounds of rips and tears as other little explosions happened all around us. I just kept waiting for it to all be over and for Morah to greet me with that look on his face.

Everything was happening at ten times the normal speed and in slow motion, all at once. We were being tossed back and forth like a chew toy in a dog's jaws. If not for somehow being strapped back into the seat belts, we would both have been thrown out of the windows by now. All we could do is yell and wait for the ride to stop or kill us. I wouldn't have made a wager either way.

And then the plane came to an instant stop and we were both thrown forward as far as the straps would allow. Instantly, the world was quiet again. No trees breaking. No engines. No screaming. Just quiet.

The plane had come to rest a few feet above the ground, hanging from what was left of the fuselage and the broken trees it had destroyed. It appeared we were on a slope and below us was a large stream or river. My ears began to work again, I could hear the water as it moved over the rocks. Well, maybe I wouldn't be seeing my old pals today after all.

I took a quick inventory to see if I was missing any limbs or if anything was broken or bleeding. I flexed my fingers and then my arms. So far, so good. I didn't see any blood dripping from me, yet, so that was a good sign. I flexed my toes, hoping they were still all there, since I couldn't immediately see my feet. After one more bend at the knees, I decided that for now, everything was intact and working.

I looked over at Sid and she was only half-conscious. She was groaning a little, but I didn't see any blood and all of her parts seemed to be in the right places so I took that as a positive sign. Glass half full, remember?

"Sid. Sid! Are you all right?" I asked, more trying to wake her up than gauge any injuries.

She gave a groan again, but her eyelids began to flutter. She woke up and instinctively grabbed the stick as her eyes went wide and she looked back and forth quickly.

"Easy. Easy......we crashed," I said in the most hopeful and comforting way I could muster, considering the present circumstances.

"No shit, Sherlock, I was there, remember?!" she said back to me, in a very ungrateful tone.

"Are you hurt?" I asked, trying to ease the tension that had somehow immediately jumped a few notches.

She looked stunned as she just stared forward, her jaw tight, as she realized she was still gripping the stick with every fiber of muscle she had. Slowly she relaxed her grip and let go of the stick. Then her face relaxed and she took a few slow breaths. She closed her eyes again, and I could tell she was trying to collect herself. Then she opened her eyes and looked at me.

"You motherfucker."

I guess she was okay.

16

Know Thy Enemy

*A*lthough Sun Tzu would not be born for a few thousand more years, he would change the world with his revolutionary take on strategy. If historians only knew who truly influenced him, they might not shower him with the avalanche of accolades he now enjoys. But we knew of those tactics long before Tzu's soul was even a wisp of thought. Today, we were going to find out what made the Draconians tick.

Morah had taken us to the center of a large landmass and we had moved among the Draconians as they came and went about their daily activities. He had explained that many beings in the cosmos shared similar physical traits although they appear vastly different from one another.

As he began to point out different parts of the lizard, information was poured into me like sunlight. The head, it's brain, the eyes, digestive system, hands, feet, nervous system. Now that I could actually see this being and how it moved and communicated, I was better able to understand the information concerning its physical makeup. It made more sense when I could put the visual of what I was seeing together with the information Morah was sending into me. If I had a physical self, I would be smiling with the joy of knowing all of these new things. I felt like a container that could never be filled and the more I had, the more I wanted. I enjoyed learning, and couldn't wait for whatever came next.

"Timlis, to learn what motivates these creatures we will visit some of them so that you may witness their conversations and how they behave. You have the ability to understand the words of all beings in the cosmos so pay attention to the sounds they make, as this is how they convey their thoughts to one another, at least for the most part," he explained.

At that point, I began to watch each being we passed and take care to understand what was coming from their mouths. Suddenly, it all began to make sense and I was equally excited and shocked at what they were conveying to one another. At home, I knew only words of love and encouragement, even when being taught, but here, there seemed to be much of the opposite. I didn't even know how to describe it.

"Morah, what are they saying to each other?" I asked, almost shocked.

"Timlis, you can understand their language as clearly as I can. What is your question? Be more precise," he said.

"They do not seem to be joyous in any way. I am not sure what this is. I have never encountered the feelings they are displaying towards each other," I said.

"There are endless degrees of different emotions that beings throughout the cosmos possess. Love and hate are at the opposite ends of this spectrum. It is these two qualities and the endless spectrum between that fuels our existence. We are here to experience, absorb, and become more whole. The lizards have few of these qualities. They operate mostly from hate and a desire to be better than the next being, whether it be its own kind, or one from another planet," he said.

I then began to listen more closely to not only their words, but how they were intended to convey information and the emotion behind it. They seemed to outwardly dislike each other. If one were to bump into another as they passed, they would make sounds and say unkind words.

"Why would the Creator make such a being, Morah?" I half-asked, half-pleaded. This seemed to make no sense to me. Why allow a being to exist which brought no good to the Creator?

"Timlis, you are thinking too small. First, there are multitudes of beings that exist throughout the cosmos that we cannot merge with and at first seem to serve no purpose to the Creator. However, how we interact with others and how they affect those around them have a direct effect on each of us, thereby causing us to learn from them, which in turn makes us more whole. Just because a rock lies on the ground does not mean we cannot learn from the rock. So goes a flower or body of water. We are shaped by whatever we come in contact with if we allow it, so do not be so quick to dismiss the opportunity to learn from each and every thing or being you are exposed to. Every moment you exist is a moment to learn," he explained.

I felt like I had gone backwards instead of forwards in my education. I was failing to see what seemed to be obvious to Morah. Perhaps I was not as smart or special as the Creator and the teachers had hoped for.

Morah again sensed my mood. "Timlis, I have been in the cosmos for a very long existence. I have been to Earth countless times, as well as other planets. I have built stones and plants and planets. I have helped to seed beings so that they might mature into greatness one day. Some did. Some did not. However, at no point, once we have started a new life, do we ever stop it from developing. We bring life, but we do not stop it, even if it becomes something different than we originally intended. It simply becomes what it was meant to be. I did not learn all of this in an instant, and neither shall you."

I pondered all of this as Morah led us to a structure and then into a room within. The room was filled with many shapes that I did not recognize but I allowed myself to simply take note of them and not worry over each one. I would let myself accept that I knew very little and I would have time to educate myself gradually. Not knowing was different than not learning. Patience was a skill.

17

Know Thy Enemy (Part 2)

The room held two of the Draconians. They were in the middle of a conversation. They did not seem happy, but truthfully, I had yet to encounter one which did. We positioned ourselves in the upper corner of the room, watching the scene unfold before us.

"This is the leader of the Draconians," Morah explained. "He makes decisions for all other beings of his kind and then has others carry out his demands. Listen now so you might understand how they speak and behave. The leader's name is Stumus and this is his second-in-command, Crumbius."

Stumus stood near a transparent wall, the view of the city below him. He simply stared outside without acknowledging Crumbius. I wondered if they were communicating without using their words somehow. Suddenly, I learned that was not the case.

Stumus leapt into the air, twisting, and came towards Crumbius, landing on top of him and causing him to fall to the floor. Crumbius was now pinned to the floor with Stumus above him, his body pushing against the other.

"You imbecile! How could I have ever put you in charge of this operation?! You are obviously devoid of enough mental power to breathe the air, let alone ensure that our forces secure and maintain control over some planet so lacking of intelligence that an infant Draconian could rule it alone! You are less than worthless." Stumus hissed, his snout nearly touching Crumbius.

Crumbius made no effort to get up or dislodge himself from his leader's weight upon him. He had a look upon his face that I would later learn was fear. Stumus simply stared at the lizard being below him, apparently making some silent decision, then he slowly stood and walked back to the transparent wall. Crumbius remained on the ground.

"Get up, you idiot! Gather your idiot staff and come up with a less idiotic plan than whatever you just failed at. I want the occupants of that planet fixed and under our control before the sun sets ten more times. If you find yourself unable to accomplish this, I suggest signing your position over to someone who can and then say your farewells to your family. Leap from our tallest building or I can personally help you off. Understood?" he hissed.

"Yes, my ruler. It shall be done!" he said as he slowly backed out of the room and the doors shut behind him. Stumus continued to look down upon the city, not showing the previous emotion. He walked to an opposite wall and pushed a piece that protruded. A voice came from the wall.

"Yes, exalted one, how may I serve you?" the voice asked.

"Connect me with Gretimus immediately," he demanded.

"Standby, my ruler," the voice said.

"You'll stand before a death squad if I'm not speaking with Gretimus this very moment!" he hissed.

I was beginning to see how these beings behave towards each other. I did not like what I was seeing. I did not feel any love or support among them. In fact, it seemed quite the opposite. I was glad we did not merge with these beings. I would not enjoy trying to learn anything while sharing anything with a Draconian.

A different voice came on the speaker.

"Exalted, Stumus, how may I serve you?" the voice, presumably Gretimus, said.

"Listen to me carefully you fool. I have given Crumbius ten solars to take charge of that tiny planet we have recently welcomed into our flock. If he is not completely in charge of it by then, you are to take command immediately. You will then have five solars to fix what he could not. Do you understand?" he spat more than asked.

"Yes, my leader, completely," he replied. "What shall I do with Crumbius?"

"If he still breathes, rectify that situation," he said and pushed the part of the wall again. The voice did not reply.

Stumus walked back to the transparent wall, and once again looked over the city. He stayed there as we left.

"Do you understand them better now Timlis?" he asked.

"Yes, Morah, I am afraid I do," I said.

18

Warm Up

Smoke began to fill the cockpit as we hung in the trees, in what was left of a previously meticulously maintained aircraft. Sid glared at me with less joy in her eyes than one might hope for. Truthfully, who could blame her. We hadn't had a lot of laughs since we met and I didn't see any coming soon. Time to fill that glass back up a little, because it was well below half-full now.

"I think that's our cue to exit," I said as the smoke became thicker. I began to unbuckle as I heard her doing the same. No sense in becoming a crispy critter after surviving a plane crash. As I turned around, I couldn't help but wince. Most of the rear of the aircraft had been torn away. Wires dangled from where the fuselage was ripped. What once looked like an aircraft that had recently come from the factory now barely resembled an aircraft at all. I tried the door but it was jammed, probably due to the twisting of the metal around the edges. I put my shoulder into it but as I gave a hard hit, the entire aircraft lurched forward, threatening to dislodge from its temporary nest. Falling the last twenty feet to the rocks below didn't seem like a great end to this ride. I looked back at Sid to see if she had any ideas.

She had apparently shifted from "pissed off" mode into "survival" mode, as I could see her expression change.

"Hang on a second," she said, like I really had much of a choice here.

She went forward again and grabbed the bag that she had brought. Apparently, she had stowed it behind her seat. She pulled it free and held it up like a prize.

"I don't know if I have enough but first we have to open that door," she said.

"Enough what?" I asked, having no idea what she was talking about.

She looked at me, then back at the bag, and then at me again.

"Look, I don't have x-ray vision. I give up, what's in the bag?" I said, with a hint of annoyance.

"Not IN the bag you ass, ON the bag!" she said, and then I saw what she was talking about. There were several bracelets hanging from the front of the bag. They were made of paracord, the same cord used to make the lines on a parachute. Lately, it had become fashionable for people to make keychains and bracelets and other nifty do-dads out of this stuff. What was extra special about paracord was how strong each strand was.

She quickly pulled off the bracelets and handed two of them to me. She pulled off the other two and tossed the bag aside. She then began unwinding the bracelets, turning them back into long strands of paracord. I took my cue and began doing the same. A few minutes later, we had several feet of cord.

"All we have to do is tie some loops in them for handholds and we can let ourselves down to the ground," she said as she began making the loops. Three minutes later we were ready to go, except for the lack of an exit.

I had a plan. The rear section of the fuselage was torn open enough for us to fit through, despite the carnage of sharp metal edges and wires. However, it seemed like a better egress than trying to hammer the door open. I peered through the hole and saw the branches of the tree currently holding us up. As large as they appeared, they didn't seem big enough to be doing the job they were currently pulling off.

"If we can toss out one of the cords and lasso that branch above us, we might be able to lower ourselves to the ground," I said.

"So, we have an *if* and a *might*. Sounds perfect. How are your wild west skills, cowboy? Wanna give it a try?" she said with just the right amount of sarcasm. I think I deserved every bit of that.

"I'll give it my best shot," I said with a grin. I gathered the cord up so that when I threw it, it would hopefully play out quickly. I looked around the cabin and spied a broken piece of panel that I tore the rest of the way off and tied to the end of the cord for some weight. I carefully made my way to the hole in the side of the plane, easy not to shift the weight too much and cause us to become dislodged. Sid held very still as the plane bounced around with every movement I made. The sounds of the branches creaking outside reminded us that our time was probably limited in this situation. I wondered if Morah or Academ were watching any of this. I'd hear about this later for sure.

I hung my arm outside the plane and gave the cord a few swings to get some momentum going then gave it one last swing as the end flew upwards, over a branch, and wrapped itself around twice.

"Yeah!" I said, just a little happy with myself. I looked back at Sid, expecting the same enthusiasm, but she just stared at me. "Oh, come on! I got that on the first try."

"You mean your first try from my destroyed plane that is currently barely hanging twenty feet high in a tree," she said. "Here, start tying these ends on to your piece."

I silently took her pieces and tied them to the piece I was holding. It looked like we had at least enough to reach the ground below. Time to vacate.

"Okay, you can go first," I said.

"Why? Because I'm a woman?" she said, with a somewhat unhappy look on her face.

"Sid, there's just no right answer, but the truth is, between the two of us, you are the lightest, so let's at least give this plan a fighting chance and let the least heavy person go first. If it holds you, hopefully, it will hold me, but if I go and break it on the first try, then that just leaves you stuck in a tree and me probably dead or too injured to be much good," I said, trying not to sound anything but logical.

It must have worked, because her face changed and her tone did too. "Oh," was all she said back to me.

Very slowly, she eased herself towards me and took hold of the first loop. She gave it a tug, kind of testing how it felt and to see if the cord was secure around the branch. She seemed satisfied. Then she hooked a second loop, further down, on to her foot, since it was going to be tough to do once she was outside. At least this first bit wouldn't be so hard. Unfortunately, she was going to have to use her hands to lower herself down once she took that first foot out of the loop. It was better than nothing.

I took the last piece of cord we didn't use and tied it to the cord attached to the tree, as high as I could.

"I'll use this piece to pull it back in after you are on the ground, that way I don't lose it completely. I don't think jumping out of the plane to the cord is a good idea," I said.

"Good thinking, MacGyver," she said.

I took that as a compliment.

She slowly started to ease herself out of the torn section of the plane. I held her hand as she maneuvered between bits of metal and wire and slowly moved more and more of her body outside the plane. I kept holding her hand to steady her, as she finally made it completely out. By the time she cleared the airplane, I was half out of the plane with her, still holding her free hand and the loose strand of cord.

Did you know that there was another name for "paracord" in the military? It's also called "550 cord" because, theoretically, one strand of this can statically hold 550 pounds of weight. Pretty awesome, right? Do you know why that is important to know? Because I weigh about 170 pounds, with all of my gear on. I bet Sid weights about 140ish. That's a combined weight of 310 pounds, which is nowhere near 550. Even though I knew all of this in the back of my head, I didn't think it was relevant to our situation until that very second.

Just as I was about to let go of Sid's hand to let her swing away from the plane, the tree decided it no longer felt obligated to hold up the aircraft anymore.

Branches snapped, metal tore and all kinds of crazy sounds began exploding around us. Sid's eyes grew large as the tree began to shift and sway. There were milliseconds to decide what to do, and thank goodness we both came to the same conclusion. Instead of letting go, I instinctively grabbed Sid's hand tighter and pushed through the hole in the fuselage as it began to fall away behind me.

From all of the sounds of metal ripping and branches breaking, I wasn't sure the tree wasn't falling down as well. Sid screamed as her grip tightened on the paracord loop and my hand, suddenly taking on a lot more weight than she was ready for. Thank goodness I was still holding on to the spare piece of cord with my other hand. For what little it was worth, I was able to at least take a few pounds of my weight off of Sid. All of this happened in about three seconds, so most of what occurred was pure reactions and not much thought. Yay for survival instincts!

We were both grunting with the strain of holding on to the paracord and each other, as we looked down to see what was left of the plane crash to the ground below us. No Hollywood explosion, just more crashing sounds and torn metal sounds as it hit the rocks, rolled thirty more feet down the mountain, smashing into more trees and tearing apart even more until it finally came to a rest.

We were both breathing heavily as we swung around, trying to hold our grips.

"Sid, I can't hold your hand or this piece of cord much longer. I'm going to try to grab another rung. Okay?" I more said than asked.

I didn't wait for an answer, because I was losing my grip and it was either grab a loop or fall. I let go of the cord and grabbed at another rung at Sid's hip level. I had barely pushed my hand into the loop when our grip failed and I hung by one hand.

I gave a little grunt as we swung around more. I reached out and grabbed Sid's leg that was in the loop, just to steady myself and take a little weight off until I could find the next loop.

"This isn't exactly the plan I was going for," I grunted out, trying to lighten the situation for half a second.

"Just find the next loop and get the hell down to the ground!" she yelled between clenched teeth.

I took a couple of deep breaths and looked down. We were hanging about twenty feet in the air. The cord reached all the way down so that was a plus. The fall to the rocks below may or may not kill us but it would sure ruin our day worse than it already was.

I saw the next rung about a foot below Sid's boot and slowly let go of her leg and reached out for the loop. My arms were beginning to burn a bit from the strain; I wasn't going to be able to keep this up all day. Sid could probably hold on for a while since she had a foothold but I was doing this with only my arms so I had to get on the ball.

"Sid, I'm going to try to let myself down. Are you okay to hold there until I'm down? I can hold the rope steady once I get to the bottom," I said.

"I really don't have much of a choice, do I?" she said.

I remembered my military training for descending a rope. I looped my leg around the cord once and wound the cord between my feet to cause some friction. It wouldn't work as well as a full-fledged rope but it would be better than doing this purely by arm strength.

Once I got the rope secured around my leg and feet, most of the weight came off my hands and arms. The burning in my muscles instantly began to subside.

"Sid, you were in the military, right?" I asked

"Jeff, this really isn't the best time for this conversation is it?" she said, adding that lovely tinge of sarcasm that I so enjoyed.

"Did you ever do ropes?" I asked

"Fuck, Jeff, that was forever ago!" she shot back.

"Look, hopefully, some muscle memory will kick in but watch what I'm doing with my legs and feet and it will make coming down way easier and safer," I said.

She looked down and as she did, I let the cord dangle between my legs again, as I slowly rewrapped my leg and made a show of how to put the cord between my feet.

"See, I'm using the cord around my leg and between my feet to take the weight off my hands and let myself down easier. There's no way we're going to get our feet in these loops to climb down. Did you see how I did that?" I asked.

"Yeah, I saw and I kind of remember doing it. Go on down and hold the rope and I'll give it a try," she said.

I lowered myself down, avoiding some of the chunks of the plane when I finally reached the ground. We were still on a fairly steep slope and there was wreckage all over the place. I doubted there would be any rescue teams responding since our grey friends are notorious for disabling transponders. Aren't they a lovely group?

I grabbed two of the loops and leaned back, letting my weight pull the cord tight.

"Okay, I'm ready when you are," I yelled up.

I could see her take a couple of deep breaths as she pulled her foot out of the loop and hung on solely with her hands. Her other hand found the loop above her head, so she was able to steady herself as she tried to wrap the cord around her right leg the way she had seen me do it.

"That's it!" I yelled, "put the cord over your foot and use your other one against it cause friction and slow you down." It was like yelling the directions on how to tie your shoe. At least she had done this at some point in her past so she kind of had the gist of it. She tried wrapping her foot a few different ways until she was satisfied she had done it correctly and began to slowly lower herself down.

Finally, one foot hit the ground and then the other. She let go of the cord and wiped her hands on her pants. She clenched and unclenched her fingers, trying to get circulation back. She slowly looked around and then down the hill, taking in the pieces left of her plane.

I was ready to get punched in the kisser but she just continued to look down the mountain.

"Crap," was all she said.

19

The Storm

"You have seen enough for now," Morah said.

Before I could comment, a mist overtook us and when it cleared, we were home. In fact, we were in the classroom, and Academ stood before us. For a moment, no one spoke, as if we were each taking in some shared knowledge.

"Timlis," Academ now spoke, "it is time for you to visit Earth for your first time."

"I don't feel ready," I said. I felt as if I were just beginning to grasp what was going on around me and what was expected of me.

"We could go on teaching you here for eternity," Morah said. "Each time you come back here, you will learn many more lessons. However, the lessons you learn while you are carnate on the Earth are equally as important. You must learn what it is to be human; how they behave, feel emotion, treat each other. You must be able to move among them with the knowledge you now possess, but never allow anyone else to ever discover your true nature or mission. If even one of them were to learn why you are there, they may alert others, and eventually the Draconians could learn of our plan. If that were to happen, they will forever be ready to fight our efforts."

"What will I do as a human?" I asked. "Do I attempt to stop the Draconians from subverting the population? I do not feel prepared."

"Your only mission during this first life is to go through the process of being born, growing up, fitting in and learning how to behave as an Earth human, which you will fully be. This is not an easy thing, Timlis," Morah said. "Watch. Learn. When you have used your time wisely and have finished what that life can give you, then you will leave and return to us."

"How does this happen?" I asked.

"Come with us," Academ said.

And with that, we traveled to another large, empty room. In the middle of the room stood a podium with different colors on top. Before us was a large, semi-circular wall that appeared to be as much mist as wall. Morah stood before the podium and began to take a form.

"I stand before you now as the representation of the last human I resembled as a carnate," Morah said. He looked wonderful. He had many of the same features as a Draconian. Arms, legs, feet and hands. His outside was not a green color, it was more brown, and he had a different head with vastly different characteristics.

"Is this how I will look as a human?" I asked.

"Most every human looks different from the next," Academ explained. "Although they share most attributes, they are dissimilar enough to be distinguishable from one another. This is one of many lessons you will learn."

"How does one become a human?" I asked.

Suddenly, the misty wall began to fill with images. I was shown one small, unhappy human emerging from another human. I watched as this small Earth creature grew and became larger and different in size. It wore colors over its skin and learned to move on its own and eventually how to interact with those around it. It learned to do tasks and make things. Its size and color changed as I watched. It found a partner and soon the partner created another human from its body. More images of its life were shown. Some were happy, some sad. Eventually, the person laid down and closed its eyes. I saw one of our souls approach the human from above as the soul of the human slowly drifted up and away from its former body. For a moment, the soul appeared lost but once it realized the other soul nearby, it became a joyous color and the two of them traveled home.

"Timlis, this journey you have just witnessed feels as if it takes a very long time to occur while you are in human form. As a new human, you are helpless for quite some time, much like you were when you were first created as a soul. You depend on those around you to help you survive and learn. Later, you are able to be more self-sufficient, and eventually, live on the terms you arranged for yourself before becoming carnate. When that life is over, you come back home. Most souls return to review the lessons they learned and what new ones they will attempt next. You, however, will not be learning those types of lessons. Instead, you will review what you have learned about the Earth's invaders and we will formulate what our next steps will be for you to remove them and fix what they have altered."

"The humans were on a path to quickly become the most thriving and intelligent beings the Creator has had the joy of accepting into this vast realm, but the Draconians, with the help of the Grey Ones, have injured this natural progression, and now threaten to destroy it completely."

"Timlis," Morah said. "You have a very long journey ahead of you. Academ and I will be by your side until this mission concludes. However, your only goal for your first trip is to watch and learn. You need not worry about the larger mission on this trip. Watch. Learn."

"When am I to leave?" I asked.

"Soon. But we have one last bit of information to give you," Academ said. "Every trip you make to Earth, you will be given several humans to assist you. These are souls who have volunteered to help you in times of need. They will be your parents, your friends, and sometimes they will be but briefly in your life when you need them. None of these souls know of your true mission. They only know that you are a special soul who has been given a task by the Creator and they must help you. As humans, they will not know of a mission, but will feel an overwhelming need to make sure you are cared for and do what you believe needs to be carried out. Do not tell them of the mission. Do you understand these things?"

"Yes," was all I could say.

"Good journey, Timlis," Morah said.

"Watch and learn......watch and learn.....watch and learn," was all I kept hearing from Academ, as her voice softly faded away and the room turned to mist.

Suddenly, I found myself above Earth, much as I had found myself above Dracon. I was moving quickly towards a large landmass. The waters surrounding the land were deep blue and green. I moved quickly through the white mists and towards the buildings that were clustered together. The land was mostly brown, with small green areas dotted here and there. I seemed to be moving towards one specific building and suddenly I was inside it, and inside of a room, looking down at a human with a very large area in its middle. From the life view I had witnessed moments earlier, I knew that a small human would soon emerge from this person.

I then began to drift towards this person until I was next to her skin, and then I passed through her and into the small person inside her. Darkness surrounded me. Instantly, I could hear her scream but the noise seemed muffled and odd. I also began to have an awareness that I had not known outside of this small human. I felt a different warmness than before and my movement felt constricted. I realized I had begun to merge with the small person and would soon come out, as I had seen happen earlier.

If I was here to learn, then this was going to be part of that lesson. Just as I had been brought forth by The Creator, I was about to emerge from this human. I could hear more noises but they were unclear due to my current surroundings. The tight area around me would become even more constricting for a few moments and then it would stop. This kept happening over and over until I felt a different movement around me and suddenly I was in a compacted space for a moment and then a blinding light. I heard more sounds and realized it was coming from me. My human was making sounds that did not sound entirely happy and I could understand why.

I was no longer in a warm and seemingly safe place. Sounds were coming at me from different directions. My view was not clear and I could only make out large patches of color and light. I was fully out of the human now and kept hearing large explosions of sound, followed by more sounds that I finally understood as talking. Morah had told me that I was capable of understanding all types of language throughout the cosmos so I tried to concentrate but my small human body kept making loud noises that were hard to hear over. My new body and I would have to learn to work together soon so we were not at odds with each other. Time. I needed to learn patience and allow my new lessons to begin.

"Welcome to Earth," seemed to echo within me, and it sounded like the voice of Morah.

Welcome to Earth, indeed.

20

I Get By…

My watched buzzed. I looked down at the incoming message. "Just landed. Should be in LV n 2hrs." All I could do was to reply with one of the preloaded messages. Hmmmm. I had four to choose from, and none would convey what I really needed to tell them so I just picked "okay" and hit send. Either I would be there or I wouldn't. We'd cross that bridge, and stream, and trail and mountain pass when we came to it.

As the crow flies, or a previously airworthy airplane, we were about sixteen miles from Leadville. However, there were also at least three large mountain ranges between here and there so following any nearby crows wasn't going to work very well but standing still wasn't helping either.

"Is there anything worth salvaging from what's left of the plane?" I asked Sid.

She looked down the hill at the pieces of wreckage littering the mountainside. She closed her eyes for a moment, maybe imagining what the plane looked like only an hour ago, or maybe wishing this was a dream and when she opened her eyes, she'd be back in Aspen, just waking up from a crazy dream.

She opened her eyes again and let out a sigh then turned her head to look at me.

"No. This was just supposed to be a quick flight to Leadville and back. I didn't pack anything for a long trip. It was just luck that I even grabbed my backpack."

Luck. I knew of no such animal. Over my many lives through the centuries, I came to learn there was no luck. Each of those random events in life were put before us for a reason. Sometimes they appeared to be good fortune and sometimes it was as if the Creator himself was dooming me, but I have learned each of these events had a reason. For others, it was to teach them a lesson, or to keep them on a proper path, but for me, it was to help me continue my mission. While Morah and Academ didn't directly appear to hand me a tool or alter some event, they were able to put options before me to give me choices but I had to pay attention and understand what I was seeing. I was sure that was happening now. Being abducted by Steve and his minions, the plane crash, meeting Sid; all of this may seem random but it was all leading me to my goal. I needed to keep my mind clear to the possibilities. That was one of the hardest lessons to learn but learn it I did.

"Okay, Leadville is about fifteen to twenty miles away, depending on the path we are able to take, so the sooner we start, the sooner we get there," I said.

"Wrong. Aspen is much closer and easier to get to. By my count, we have three mountain ranges to Leadville and one to Aspen. I choose one," Sid countered.

This wasn't going to be easy but I was used to that. Nothing about this mission had ever been easy. Why start today?

"Look, Sid, I have some people to meet back in Leadville in a few hours. It's important that I reach them. I wouldn't have paid you so much for such a short flight if this wasn't urgent. It's safer if we stick together and I'm heading that way. I know it's going to take longer and it's a harder haul, but there are plenty of trails on these mountains so we should be able to pick one up soon and get into Leadville before nightfall," I said.

I had given up on the idea of meeting the team on time. We had a chance to make it to Leadville before dusk, but that was if we left now and kept a steady pace. These mountains were no joke but people climbed them daily so they weren't dangerous, just large and steep. Hopefully my Garmin would hold out long enough to keep us moving in the right direction and allow me to drop messages to the crew now and then.

"That's a bad idea. We don't have any food or water and walking over three mountains isn't my idea of a good time. I'm going back. Come with me or not," she said, in a rather defiant tone.

"I know you're pissed off about the plane....," I started.

"PISSED OFF?!!!! PISSED OFF!!!!???? I passed PISSED OFF before we hit that first tree! Why did you pick my airplane?! Why did I have to be standing out there? Why did I have to say yes? Fuck! Fuck! Fuck!" she screamed, then crossed her arms and closed her eyes again. Then she whispered, more to herself than me, "You ruined my fucking life."

I could explain all of this to her, but she wasn't looking for answers this second. She was in the zone, the super pissed off, angry zone and every answer and explanation wouldn't mean shit right now. I just let her breathe and hoped it would pass soon. Sid was with me here and now for a reason, so I had to accept that and move us forward.

"I'll buy you a new plane. It can be the exact same plane or anything you want, short of a military jet fighter. I'll also triple the pay I was going to give you but I need to get to Leadville, and we need to leave right now," I said.

"Who the fuck are you, Jeff?" she said. "You're dressed like you just got doing some local 5K, but you know how to fly planes, talk to aliens and use laser beams. What the hell is going on?" she said, choking back tears.

"First, my name isn't Jeff, it's Jim. We have several hours of walking ahead of us to Leadville. We have a much better chance of getting there in one piece together than separately. I'll fill you in on what's going on while we walk and you'll have plenty of answers. Right now all you need to hear is that I have plenty of money and I need to meet some people soon," I said, as she stared blankly at me.

"Are you some kind of terrorist or nut job or just a crazy rich guy?" she asked.

"No. Come on, Sid, let's get moving and I'll tell you what you need to know," I said as I started down the mountain, towards Leadville.

She looked up the mountain then back down. She let out a breath she probably didn't know she was holding and started down the rocky landscape behind me. Off to Leadville we went.

21

Naqadah

*B*ecause this all started so long ago, at least from a human perspective, you can't ignore the historical aspect of this story. However, this is absolutely not a history lesson. I jumped into different time periods to learn, to search, and to plan how to reverse what the lizards and greys had begun. They had a large head start on me so this was going to take a good while to unravel and straighten out but time was a luxury to me. I didn't have to think in terms of months, years, or even a lifetime. I could play this out carefully and do it right but every marathon begins with that first step and so far, I was just putting my socks on.

This was not the warm and soft environment I had experienced as a newly made soul. The noises around me were nearly overwhelming. Many people all speaking at the same time and through the hole in the wall I kept glimpsing flashes of light and deafening booms afterwards. Later, I would find out that Morah had arranged a display of lightning for my arrival, complete with an earth-shattering thunderstorm. Morah had a stoic sense of humor laced with symbolism that I would come to appreciate over the eons, but on this day, it was just scary.

The others in the room during my birth were all females. They were talking quickly and at the same time, which made it hard to follow any single conversation. I was passed to one woman, who was pouring liquids over my skin. I was feeling sensations from the air and liquids I hadn't experienced as a soul before. I supposed that this was just the beginning of all of the things I would learn as a newly formed human. One thing I had to get under control was the screaming; this new baby human would not stop. He and I were not fully merged and we needed to get on the same plan sooner rather than later. Time to stop being an observer and begin being a participant.

I remembered the soft sounds from my own nursery and how it soothed me and made me feel loved and safe. In my mind, I tried to recreate that sound and concentrate on making it my single thought. I pictured my nursery and hoped all of these images and sounds were being shared with my human. Slowly, it seemed to work. The baby stopped crying and began making little sounds that I hoped meant it was happy. The human females all seemed pleased by the baby's new demeanor so perhaps our merging was beginning to take place. Eventually, if all went as planned, we would become a single unit and stay that way for many earth years. Hopefully.

The woman holding me had wrapped something around my body so all of my limbs were constricted. That was probably a good thing because not only did it feel warm and comforting, but my human and I did not seem to have any control over our new arms and legs and they flailed about on their own accord. I hoped this was a temporary situation which we would master together, but right now, being somewhat restricted was a blessing. The woman gave us to our mother who had just birthed us. She looked into our eyes and as we looked back into hers, other feelings began to stir within me I had not known before. I had known the feeling of love before but now it was evident that I was staring into the eyes of love itself. What an amazing sensation! She began to hum and I felt as if I were back in the nursery all over again.

For a moment, I stopped worrying about the mission and simply allowed myself to experience this. I could stay like this forever.

It was then that I realized this was the very feeling that the lizards were slowly destroying. Eventually, if they continued to combine with the humans, souls could no longer come to earth and merge with humans. We would not have the chance to experience looking into a mother's eyes and being consumed by the raw emotion of overwhelming and unconditional love. What a waste that would be. That one feeling alone was worth the fight.

And then something very human happened: we fell asleep, at least my human did. Suddenly, I knew for sure we were not completely bonded yet because I was able to leave his little body and float away, back into my soul form. I felt immediately liberated and concerned at the same time. Would I be able to place myself back into my human when he awoke? Needing to immediately know, I approached his body and slowly allowed myself to once again enter his body. Still asleep. I gave myself permission to leave him and once again found myself floating away from him. Would I be able to do this forever or just when he was in this small form? Time would tell, I supposed. It seemed there were plenty of lessons Morah and Academ left for me to discover for myself. I wondered what they were thinking as I floated in and out of my human.

I decided to test the boundaries of my ability and explore. I hovered above my mother and the other women, taking in the scene. My mother was holding me, still making the humming noises and gently swaying me back and forth. The other women were watching this scene, with what seemed like kind expressions on their faces.

I drifted through the building. It was filled with great numbers of items that I could not identify. More education awaited me. There were also several male humans. I wondered if one of these men were my father. They wore colorful items over different parts of their bodies. Less than the women. They also had shiny pieces around other parts.

As I listened to the conversation, I felt as if one man in particular was being singled out by the rest. Each of the men were approaching him and telling him of his great fortune by having a healthy son. I supposed they were speaking of me. They each gave my father an item of some type and he seemed happy. If these humans were my first mother and father, I was in a very good environment to learn.

Much later I would learn that Morah and Academ had planned my parents long ago. The souls who were now my parents had volunteered for this task and without knowing the details, would help me learn what it is to be human. On later missions, I would help in the process of who I was with and where I would be, but on my very first visit I had very little to plan.

I drifted upwards now, out of the building that was to become my home. I floated down the streets, watching people move about. There was light coming from many small sources and darkness most everywhere else. The planet had not turned enough for its sun to light this portion yet so it seemed people made their own light. It was so very different from Draconia. Not better or worse, but different. While the Draconians did not seem to possess the love and warmth of the humans, they appeared to be on a different level as far as their outward abilities. They did not move about in the sky or in other shapes. They did not have buildings that were so high they threatened to pierce the sky.

However, from their conversations and their actions, they seemed perfectly capable of having and using all of those things the Draconians already possessed. What a sadness it was for one race to purposely rule another one. If they treated each other in this manner, other races of beings would not have a chance, unless they somehow were able to advance themselves as well as, or beyond the Draconians. I supposed, in the end, that would be my ultimate mission.

Suddenly, I felt a yearning within me. One like I had never experienced before, as if some part of me were missing and needed replaced. If this was pain then I wanted no part of it. My immediate urge was to return to my human form. I nearly instantly reappeared in my mother's room and moved quickly towards my body, which seemed to be waking up.

The baby cried and he seemed inconsolable. We looked at our mother as she looked down at us. The other women stood around her. She moved part of the colorful items from her body and as she exposed part of herself, my human seemed to know exactly what to do. We latched onto our mother's body and began to take part of her into us. Immediately, I knew this was the yearning I had felt so strongly. My human needed to take this into us to make us feel whole again. The room fell silent as we looked back into our mother's eyes and ate, a brand new experience for both of us.

"The city of Naqadah's newest son will be strong," one of the women said. They all seemed to agree. A short time later, he was asleep again, and this time, I stayed with my human in our mother's arms. Warm. Loved.

22

Walk of Life

For the first fifteen minutes we walked in silence. I was in my own head, calculating distances and times. I imagine Sid was making her own list of things to do. Hopefully, bashing me in the face wasn't one of those things. I was sure that we were together for a reason but for the moment, I was also sure she regretted the second I came into her life. Finally, she broke the silence.

"I think it's time you fill me in," she said. She sounded calm now. Maybe that's what she had been doing for the last fifteen minutes, calming down enough to have a sensible conversation. I had been responsible for several bad things happening to her in a very short period of time. I owed her some answers, but as always, I had to dance through the minefield of facts to give the right answers. However, I'd been doing this so long, I was pretty good at painting this picture.

"Let me start by telling you something that is obvious," I said, trying not to sound condescending. "The more you know about me and what I'm doing, the more danger you are in. Information was the only reason we were taken and the more you knew, the more danger you were in. They won't stop until they get what they want, so at best, we just bought ourselves some time."

"I think you need to back up your story and start from the beginning," she said, trying to keep the obvious frustration out of her tone. "I'm a big girl and I can decide for myself how much trouble I intend to expose myself to. So I'm asking for as much information as I can get. If these flying fuckers come back after me, I want to know what I'm up against so I can be prepared."

That was fair. Now that alien lizard Steve knew about Sid he might want to have future conversations with her, assuming the bisected bastard was still breathing. Arming her with as much intel as possible, without spilling the beans on "the big picture" seemed like a reasonable and acceptable risk. Better to err on the side of caution. Not so long ago, governments learned that compartmentalized information is the best way to run a large operation and I employed this on a daily basis. Minimizing exposure to people and plans is a time tested strategy and once I learned it, I became a master.

"Seeing as how we have several hours of hiking ahead of us, we have plenty of time to talk," I said.

"I guess the gist of it is this, Sid. I am searching for something that the aliens want. While I don't know exactly where the something is, I believe I know where to find the information which will hopefully point me in the right direction. Kind of like the map room in *Raiders of the Lost Ark*. I believe the aliens think I already know where the mystery thing is. That's why they abducted me, and by accident, you. They saw their opportunity to do a snatch and grab and unfortunately, you happened to be sitting in the wrong place at the wrong time. I'm guessing they think we are working together and you have information they want as well. Questions?" I asked.

"Okay, that was some tip-of-the-iceberg crap," she said. "Who do you work for? How do you have so much money? Tell me more about the aliens, and stop dancing around the *ship*, since I heard you discussing that with them. Whose ship? What kind of ship? Why do you both want the ship?" she blurted out.

"Okay, one at a time. Let's see, who do I work for? Rather than lie to you I'll just be blunt. I can't tell you, or rather, I won't tell you, at least not right now. Let me tell you who I don't work for. I don't work for the government, any government. I don't work for some secret spy organization and I don't work for any terrorist groups. If I had to give an answer, I'd say that I'm an independent contractor," I said.

"Second, the easiest answer to the money question is this. I'm a wise investor and I have been doing it for a long time."

"Third, the aliens, let's circle back to them at the end, since they are the most complicated. The ship. The ship is an alien ship that crashed thousands of years ago. However, it still contains technology that is eons ahead of what humanity has at this time. I want to find it, so I can help humans against the aliens, and the best way to do that is to become equal or superior to them technologically. They've discovered I know about the ship and want to stop me. Their problem is, they don't know where the ship is either. It isn't one of theirs, so although they have known about its existence, they have never known its location."

"Wait a second," she said, "you're telling me that there is a crashed UFO out there somewhere and you're trying to find it so we can win a war against aliens?"

"Basically, yup," I said.

"So you think you're Indiana Jones or acting out *Independence Day* or some bullshit like that?" she said, with an ocean full of sarcasm.

"Normally, this would sound pretty crazy, but let me remind you of what happened to you over the last couple of hours. Plane in a vortex? Alien abduction? Foot sliced off and then new foot? Ring any bells?" I said, adding my own hint of sarcasm.

She was silent for a minute. "Okay," was all she said.

"Okay?" I asked. "Okay? I thought you'd have some snarky comeback."

"Well, Jeff, uh, I mean Jim, or whoever you really are, it's hard to argue with all the crazy shit that's gone on since we left Aspen. So what can you tell me about the asses who snatched us out of my plane," she said.

"Well, you obviously saw there were two different types. The first one is a "grey". They really are exactly right out of the movies and all the information out there. They have teamed up with the other aliens for mutual reasons. The greys are masters at snatch and grab and the other aliens have a more sinister agenda."

"The second alien, who I called Steve, is actually not a human. He's a Draconian and in his normal skin, he looks like a huge lizard. Like many different animals here on Earth, he can change how he looks. It's part of his genetic abilities. However, he can't just do this instantly, like some Hollywood movie. It's a process that takes a few hours. The Draconians are a dangerous group and have no problems with torture and murder to get what they want. As far as I know, the greys have never killed anyone, although some of the people they have abducted may have wished they would have," I said.

"So, Steve is a lizard alien, not a human?" she asked.

"Yup, Steve is a big ol', green-skinned, stubby tailed, snouted, mean-ass lizard," I said.

Sid just shook her head, trying to absorb all of this. It was a lot to take in all at once. I really wasn't telling her information other humans hadn't already put together for themselves, although most had the big picture wrong. Either way, lots of humans knew of these aliens and that they were up to no good, which is enough.

"Fuck," was all she said, as we both continued through the forest. It took her a few minutes to process all of this before she had more questions.

"So, to sum this up, you are a super-rich dude who is on a mission to save the human race from some evil aliens?" she said.

"Well when you put it that way, it just sounds stupid," I said with a huge goofy smile on my face.

"Yeah, well, I think that movie has already been made, but seeing is believing, so I really don't have much of an argument. Really, I'm just waiting for BigFoot to step out and offer to have high tea with us," she said.

"Don't get me started on BigFoot," I said, with a fun smile on my face.

She didn't even ask.

23

Walk Like an Egyptian

*A*s it turned out, Morah had placed me in an average Egyptian family to learn what being a human was like. For those keeping score, it was approximately 3000 BC/BCE/ABCDEFG. As a history lesson, volumes of books could be, and have been, written on what life was like back then. It was vastly different from today's society but at the same time, incredibly similar. People are people and they have always been motivated by the same goals, which make them behave in expected ways. They speak different languages, they dress differently, but at the end of the day, they want to eat, drink and stay alive. However, documenting different cultures wasn't my goal. My objective was simple. Learn how to use a body. Learn how humans behaved. Fit in. Observe. Saving the world was not on my list of things to do quite yet. One day, but not this time out.

I'd be remiss if I didn't mention some of my first challenges as a newbie. Talking was number one. I knew exactly what my parents and those around me were saying. In fact, that was also one of my first mistakes. Those around me seemed to notice

that I had a look about me that conveyed my
ability to grasp their speech long before most
humans of that age. That would come in handy
next time. My problem learning to talk had to do
with my human host body. While I knew what I
wanted to say to my caretakers, the vocal abilities
of my baby body weren't quite up to the task. The
more we merged into one entity, the better we got
but those first few months were frustrating.

As much as I wanted to speak to my parents
there really wasn't much to tell them. They took
care of most every need someone of my age
could ask for. We were fed, clothed, bathed, and
cleaned when our body eliminated its food and
drinks. I observed all of this with a great degree of
fascination. We had none of these issues as a
soul but that was one of the many reasons for
becoming a human. Learning and experiencing. I
could certainly begin checking off those boxes,
even though it didn't directly pertain to my
mission.

Eventually, we started forming some words,
which pleased and delighted everyone around us.
It was peculiar how excited our parents were to
hear us talk. (I'm going to have to start referring to
myself as a single unit since *we* eventually
became more of a *me*). The Egyptian language is
one of my favorites, even today. The words
seemed more expressive and more interesting.
I'm sorry I have few people to speak with during

my current life that might actually understand it. However, I still get a kick from going to museums and reading the hieroglyphs as easily as ever. The Creator gave me a wonderful memory.

Walking. Oh boy, what a hard one the first time! My big baby head didn't help my center of gravity and the tiny feet weren't any better. The process was the same as it is to this very day. It's a study in trial and error, weighing heavily on the error side. After many scrapes, bruises and seeing my blood for the first time, I was able to master putting one foot in front of the other. Future lives would have me being careful not to grasp this too fast out of the gate but being carried around by someone else isn't such a bad thing. Especially when short, baby legs can't really move you great distances very fast.

After walking and talking, just learning the social structure of the community was the next largest task. You had to understand what was expected of you and behave in a normal fashion. My first time as a human taught me this valuable lesson. While I was leaps and bounds ahead of humans my own age, I had to work not to draw attention to myself. One piece of advice given to me from Academ was to never stand out from the crowd too much. The lizards were always on the lookout for leaders and those who stood out. They would try to subdue or subjugate those people to keep them from ever becoming too powerful. I constantly reminded myself to fit in. I made errors on purpose and did my best to appear average. At least never good enough to bring unwanted eyes glaring my way.

As I grew older, I had my first encounter with the aliens. Our society was built around a cult-like religion called *Set*, if religion is even the right word. Set was the god of chaos but I had only seen drawings of him. He was depicted as a man's body and a head like an ugly dog or aardvark. This was either someone's wild imagination or our friends from the stars. I soon found out.

As I had learned from my parents and the older ones, the gods would make an actual appearance occasionally to give us jobs to do and commands to heed to keep us on the right path. Mostly, they came to collect the gold we had mined for them. On the much anticipated day, they showed up and didn't mind making a large spectacle of themselves.

They openly used their alien ships, flying through the sky and flashing lights and producing sounds. While I knew they were just the ships they traveled from other planets with, it was no less impressive to see it as a human for myself. It certainly had the desired effect upon the masses. Fear. People dropped to their knees and worshipped the ships and those inside as they eventually landed on the ground.

As expected, Set himself made an appearance, although I imagined any of the lizards could turn itself into a passable Set. He came strolling out of his ship with great ceremony, along with several other lizards who had taken on various other shapes to amaze and frighten the population. I bet this would even work on a great deal of the population today despite how technologically advanced we imagine ourselves.

Set was led away by our priest to the building where we stored the masses of gold our people had been tasked to extract from the nearby mines. For as long as anyone could remember, our alien gods had commanded us to provide them with as much gold as we could pull from the earth. Every few years, on a particular date, they would come and take the fruits of our labor. In return, they would not kill us or allow other mean and nasty gods to harm us. Not knowing these gods were merely folks from another planet who were using their advanced technology to pull the wool over the sad human's eyes, no one questioned them.

Who would? I mean, they did just show up in some flying chariot. They did look like humans with animal heads. And when it came time to move several tons of gold into their ships they didn't wait for our sorry Egyptian asses to slowly carry the heavy metal into their waiting rides; they levitated the gold in a magical, god-like show of awe and amazement. Very impressive.

All the while I took mental notes. I tried to observe as much as I could concerning their ship, just in case I needed that information one day. I also watched their manners and the way they treated each other and the humans they came in contact with. It was classic lizard mentality.

After loading their bounty, they entered the great hall of the priests, where they would dine and issue new commands. A short time later, we all watched as they exited the hall and strutted back to their fire chariots. Before entering their craft, Set turned to address the masses. He announced that we had met our goals during this visit but commanded us to double our efforts before their next visit or fire would rain from the sky. They all turned around together, as if they had practiced this move a hundred times, and made their way inside. Even the door closing behind them looked impressive. They left in an equally spectacular display of superiority. Shock and awe was as real then as it is now. They made several low passes over the heads of the people, causing as much panic as astonishment. People ran in every direction and frightened goats shit everywhere. Some people probably did too.

As amazed as everyone seemed, they were equally relieved that our gods had left their minions. I was feeling more angry than anything else. Not only were the lizards destroying the humans' ability to merge with souls but they were using us as slave labor. Why did they want gold? That seemed odd. If they wanted gold, weren't they smart enough to extract it themselves? I had questions and knew I would eventually have my answers, either in this life or between Earth lifetimes.

Everyone slowly went back to their daily rituals and routines. I hurried home. I wanted to discuss this visit with my parents, who had seen this display two or three times before. Now that I had seen this for myself, they might be able to fill in some gaps. If I was eventually going to beat these creatures, I needed to know more about them.

24

SOLD

We continued to walk through the forest at the best speed we could manage. We hadn't found a trail yet so going around boulders, threading through trees and crossing the occasional stream was slowing us down. Sid hadn't spoken for quite a while. She seemed lost in her own thoughts, which was fine with me, the less I had to explain, the better. I wasn't going to lie to her, but throwing up roadblocks to her questions had gotten both of us frustrated. Eventually, she just stopped asking.

"Okay, I'm in," she finally said.

"I don't remember asking you to join anything," I said, but with a smile on my face.

"Jim, do all of your friends know how hilarious you are or do you just do that for me?" she asked.

"Who says I have friends?" I said.

"Okay, let's get off the merry go round. I'm already in whatever is going on, so me just saying it out loud is just acknowledging what we both already know. Since your alien friends are looking for both of us now, I might as well see this through instead of just waiting around to get beamed back up and probed," she said.

I really couldn't argue any of that, since it was all true. Also, she seemed capable and not easily detoured by outlandish information so that really did make for a good teammate. I had looked for specific talents to assemble the team I presently had but Sid seemed to fall into my lap, even though I knew those kinds of things didn't actually happen. Sid had obviously agreed to help me while between lives and Morah and or Academ had placed her in the right place at the right time. Coincidences really didn't happen. Now we just had to figure out what part of the puzzle she fit into.

"Okay, Sid, you're in," I said. "What do we need to do about your previous employment to tie up any loose ends?"

"You can still make that right later. That is my company and was my plane. I sunk everything I had into it so if you are as good as your word, you can fix that after our mission is complete," she said.

"Our mission?" I asked, with a whimsical smile. "I don't think you know what you're getting yourself into here, Sid."

"Look, you were right, I was in the Air Force. There were plenty of times we were sent on missions where we knew less than half of the facts but we knew enough to get the job done. I understand how that works so you don't have to dance around stuff you can't tell me. Just give me the *need to know* line and I'm good. Okay?" she said.

And this is how it always worked. When someone accepted their role to come to Earth to help me, they were never hard to convince. Like Sid, they seemingly accepted their part blindly but that wasn't true. Before even being born, they had known they would spend some or all of their lives helping me with a mission that was approved by the Creator himself so when it came time to get things done, I didn't have to try very hard to convince them to join.

"So, who are these people you're meeting in Leadville? Why Leadville anyway? Where are you from anyhow, and is Jim your real name? Oh, and also, why do you keep saying humans like you're not human? Are you some kind of lizard too?" she spat out all at once.

"Geez, Sid! Have you been thinking up all of these questions for the last thirty minutes?" I asked.

"Well, yeah," she said.

"We're going to Leadville to meet the rest of the team. There are four other people and if we find our way out of this forest, I'll make introductions. We're in Leadville because I'm running the Leadville 100. It's a 100 mile ultramarathon that starts Saturday morning. Yes, my real name is Jim, and yes, I am 100% human," I answered.

"I thought you were on some ship finding mission so why are you running a 100 mile ultramarathon? And for that matter, why the hell would anyone run 100 miles?" she asked.

"I do races like this across the country when the place I need to go corresponds with a race. I use the race as my cover so I blend in. A place like Leadville doesn't have many visitors, and if I just showed up I'd look completely out of place and questions would be asked. But during this race event, thousands of people show up and I just become a grain of sand on the beach. Races like this usually require a team, or crew, who come along to help the runner, so my people fit in easily and don't look out of place."

"As to why anyone would run 100 miles, I guess each person has their own reasons. I do it because I can, it's fun and it fits in with accomplishing my mission. Total win in all categories!" I said.

"We're in Leadville because rumor has it that hidden in one of these mine shafts is information that will lead us to where we can find the lost alien ship. Long ago, and still to this day, the aliens didn't always play nice with each other. Occasionally, a fight would break out and someone would lose. During one particular battle, a ship was damaged and crashed. Some of the occupants were able to escape. Somehow, one or some of those aliens made it to Leadville, where they were able to live undetected in subterranean systems. Before the last one died, they left information as to where that ship had crashed. The aliens who shot them out of the sky were the lizards but they were never able to find the damaged ship. I have no idea how they discovered I was hunting the ship but they believe I know where it is, hence, I was kidnapped and you came along for the ride. Make sense?" I asked. My mouth was getting dry from all of the talking.

"Yeah, but how did you find out about the aliens in Leadville and that there might be a clue to the ship here?" she asked.

"Over the last several years, with the help of the National UFO Reporting Center's online database, I was able to follow-up on several reported cases. Leadville was unique for several reasons. It's the highest incorporated city in the United States. It has a mining system that boomed in the late 1800s and played out. And finally, it had a woman named Elizabeth "Baby Doe" Tabor who lived in the town, and refused to leave the mine until her dying day, even though she was destitute and had no reason to be there. All of these facts in themselves seem completely unconnected until you take each one and begin to explore a bit deeper," I said as I began to explain the mystery.

"Even though the UFO sightings are documented online, there have been tales of UFOs visiting this area for as long as there have been humans around to report it. Native Americans would tell stories of the lights in the sky and the flying horses. This tells me that our friends in the skies are around here looking for something."

"As far as it's altitude, I think whoever hid what we are looking for chose a place they thought would be desolate enough that humans wouldn't be attracted to stay here in large numbers. That alone isn't a big clue but the next part adds credibility," I explained, having fun spinning the tale.

"Jim, I've been to Leadville before. I've taken the tours and heard the story of Baby Doe before but there aren't any UFO stories listed or did I miss that part of the tour?" she asked, with sarcasm turned up to about eight.

"No, you're right, but I'm not done yet, padawan. So, instead of people rarely coming here, miners were desperate to look under every rock and root as they made their way out West, and in 1860, prospectors struck gold just south of downtown Leadville. That put an end to desolation and in poured the people."

"A few years later, a man named Horace Tabor buys the Matchless Mine. He and his beautiful wife, Elizabeth, become astronomically rich. You can read the whole story for yourself, but in the end, the money went away and Horace died, but before he did, he begged Elizabeth to hold on to the Matchless, which she did until they found her dead in her shack of a house, which sat next to the mine, in 1935."

"Now, while this makes for an interesting story, it's the next bit that makes me think a clue to the ships location awaits us in Leadville. Have you ever been to the Silver Dollar Saloon?" I asked, with a smile on my face.

"Sure, anyone who goes to Leadville visits that place. Every legendary gunfighter and outlaw from the old west called that place home for some period of time so it's practically a tourist trap," she said.

"Did you see the picture of "Baby Doe" hanging on the wall," I asked.

"Yeah, so?" she said.

"What most people see in that picture is an attractive woman, dressed in the clothes of a wealthy person of the time, wearing expensive jewelry. But what I see is an attractive woman, dressed in the clothes of a wealthy person of the time, wearing a necklace that resembles ones worn by the aliens who were rumored to have been shot down all those thousands of years ago." I said.

"Jim, how exactly would you know what kind of necklace an alien would have been wearing when it crashed thousands of years ago?" she asked.

Good question. How to explain this without giving away the farm. Easy.

"Sid, it's one of those details where you're going to have to trust me. If you stay on this team and become part of this mission, you're going to have to trust me on stuff like this. Remember, the more you know, the more our lizard friends will be able to yank out of your grey matter. Kapish?" I said.

"Kapish," she said, with a bit of a sour look on her face.

25

P/2004 R3

I *was eight-years-old during my first encounter*
with the lizard gods in Naqadah. After speaking
with my parents, I discovered that they made
an appearance on a regular time schedule every
seven and one-half years during the arrival of the
comet Set. They didn't call it a comet at the time.
They believed it was Set's ship lighting up the
heavens and knew once it made it's arrival, Set
would show up within a few days. Today, we
know this comet as P/2004 R3 and it shows up
every 7.52 years. I'll probably never know why the
lizards picked that event to let the people know
they would soon show up. Maybe it's how they did
it on all of the other planets and since it worked to
help support the myths and legends, it was a
good tool. That's just my guess. I was too young
to experience their first arrival, and the second
one caught me mostly off guard but I'd be ready
the next time.

Since I had a few more years until the next
great visitation, I used my time to become better
at being human and to learn about the lizards.
Most boys would start working at the mines at the

age of ten. Initially, you would do easy jobs that would make life for the actual miners more tolerable. Fetching food and water and passing information is where you started. I decided that if I wanted to learn more about our gods then the mines would be a great start. I told my parents that I was ready to do my part in the mines and to speak with the right people to make that happen. Within a week, I had my job. I was told to report to a man named Nebetka. Early that morning, I left my home as the sun was just beginning to rise. I was excited to actually be working on my mission even though that wasn't my real objective. However, I'd already settled into a life as a regular human boy so boredom was creeping in quickly. If I had to live another 800 years or more at this pace, I felt like I would be wasting my time. Learning to be a human took less time than I imagined, or at least it seemed that way. I was sure that there were more lessons to learn as an adult but I had the main bits conquered. I laughed, cried, got angry and had fun all at the appropriate times and didn't seem to stand out above or below anyone else. I appeared average in every way, which was exactly what I wanted to be.

When I showed up at the mine, Nebetka was an easy man to find. He was the one doing all of the yelling and none of the working. This would be a theme for the ages as far as finding who a supervisor was at a job. Just look for the guy not sweating.

I stopped behind Nebetka as he was telling a worker how worthless and lazy he was. The worker looked terrified, mostly because Nebetka said he would report this worker to Set himself the next time he arrived. Even at eight years old, I knew this was a lie. Finally, after the worker was dismissed, Nebetka took notice of me, but with less than a kind look.

"Go away, there is work to be done and you have no place here," he spat.

"I am Sabaf (my Egyptian name this life), son of Merkha. I was told to report to you for my work assignment," I said.

He looked me up and down, which wasn't very far considering my eight-year-old body. He kept the same disgusted look on his face that he had with the lazy worker. Maybe that was the face he had all of the time or he was just mad when his eyes were open. Either way, he wasn't delighted to see me.

"You are too small. Go home and come back when you are big enough to actually work," he said as he turned away from me.

"I'm big enough to take food and water to the workers and I'm stronger than any of the other boys I see working now," I said.

"Go home," he said, this time not even turning to look at me.

"I will work for seven days with no pay. If I do not do a good enough job for you, I will gladly leave," I said. I hoped giving him a free worker might cause him to rethink his decision.

He crossed his arms and seemed to be in thought for a few moments. This appeared to be a hopeful sign.

"Bring water to the workers near the entrance to that mine," he pointed to a mine, "and do not go anywhere else. If I see you anywhere else, doing anything else, you will go home with fewer teeth than you came here with. Do you understand?" he sneered.

"Yes, Nebetka, I will be a good worker," I said.

Without asking, I ran to the large jugs of water which had been brought from the river. I loaded several smaller ones on sticks the way I had seen other boys doing earlier. With the stick across my shoulders and the jugs on the sticks, I began to make my way to the mine. This was my first encounter with manual labor, but unfortunately, it wouldn't be my last. However, it was one step closer to getting near to those people who knew more about the mines and why the lizards wanted gold. Information was my real payment and I would work hard to keep this job and find my answers.

26

Jon

We continued on, down one valley and up another, not yet finding a well-beaten path. It was beginning to be early evening, and by all estimations we were going to be spending the night in the woods. There was just no making good time in a heavily wooded forest with steep terrain. At least we had the occasional stream to drink from.

We broke out of the wood line into a small meadow, like we had a few times before. This time, I saw a mirage. Sitting in the meadow, still as a picture, was a small helicopter. I looked back at Sid, to see if she was seeing the same thing I was. Yep, she had a look of pure disbelief on her face. Okay, maybe this was a real helicopter.

As we approached, I noticed the words, *Leadville Sightseeing Tours* written on its side, and a familiar face staring back at me as he leaned against the small chopper. It was Jon.

"Took ya long enough," he said.

"Man, you're a sight for sore eyes," I said back with a huge grin on my face. "You're amazing, Jon! I can't wait to hear how you found us."

"Who's your friend?" he asked, staring over my shoulder at Sid.

"This is Sid. Sid, this is Jon," I said, making proper introductions.

"Glad to meet you, Sid." he said, "That's our pilot, Tony, who I just met a few hours ago and who will be taking us back to Leadville as soon as we pile in. You didn't make any more friends on your way did you? This thing only holds four."

"Nope, just Sid," I said. "So, how exactly did you find us?"

"We'll discuss that on our way back to Leadville, but for now, we have three other teammates waiting for us at the Tennessee Pass Café with hot food and cold beers so let's not keep them waiting any longer. Sound good, Sid?" he asked with a smile on his face.

"I don't know you, Jon, but I sure like all the stuff you're saying! Let's get the hell out of here. I could use a few beers with the day I've had," she said.

"Yeah, it's been one of those days, Jon. Let's go. I'll fill you in after the second beer is ordered," I said with a wink.

Tony fired up the rotors as we opened the doors to pile into the tiny helicopter.

"Howdy, everyone," Tony shouted above the sounds of the engines, "strap in and put your headphones on. We'll make introductions once were in the air. Momma's got dinner on the table and I'm hungry as a hibernating bear so let's get moving."

Sounded good to me. Breakfast this morning seemed like a lifetime ago and I was looking forward to whatever was put on the plate.

Once we cleared the trees, Tony started the introductions, "Hi, I'm Tony and I'll be your pilot for this very brief trip back to Leadville. I've already met Jon, so who's in the back seat?" he asked.

"Hi, Tony, I'm Jim and this is Sid. Thanks loads for the rescue. I'd about had enough of the nature walk. Hope we didn't make you miss a hot dinner," I said.

"Nah, Momma will keep it in the oven if I'm late. She knows what pays the bills so she's always happy when I can get a flying gig, especially one that pays this well!" he said with a smile on his face and a glance to Jon.

Jon turned from the front seat to look back at me.

"Tony didn't mind being paid in cash so I hope that's okay with you," he said.

"Jon, I don't even want to know. Everyone is safe and we're on our way to food and beer. As long as we don't encounter any more side trips today, money is the least of my worries," I said.

"Amen to no more side trips!" Sid chimed in.

Tony raced the helicopter through the mountain passes at a few hundred feet above the trees. Flying a helicopter at this altitude couldn't be easy but Tony seemed to be more than capable. I made a mental note of Tony and his helicopter. You never know when services like this might come in handy in the future. Specialized services are always welcome in this venture. I could tell Sid was glancing around, looking for unwanted spacecraft to come zooming by. I couldn't blame her. Truthfully, I probably do that and just never noticed. We all fell silent for the remainder of the flight. Mostly because we all knew that Tony wasn't part of the team and it wasn't wise to speak freely in front of strangers, even those who are saving your butt.

The airport came into view soon and Tony maneuvered to a pad near a hangar that had his company name and logo above the giant doors. The sun was just starting to push towards the tops of the mountains and dusk would soon be upon us.

As the chopper touched down and the rotors began to spin down, Tony unbuckled and shut down the rest of the electronics. That was our cue to exit. We hung up our headsets and stepped out of the helicopter.

"I'd love to stay and chat but this has already been a long day," Tony said. "If you need my services again, Jon knows how to contact me." We all shook hands and then Tony took off at a good clip towards his hangar.

"I have our car in the parking lot on the other side of the hangar," Jon said as he started in that direction.

"Jon, Jim, we need to swing by the office here to let them know that I'm alive and well. I was supposed to land here hours ago and if they don't hear from someone soon, they're going to start asking questions and making calls," Sid said with a bit of concern on her face.

We walked inside the flight office and Sid knew right where to go. Apparently she had been here enough times that she knew the guys behind the desk.

"Sid! You should have been here hours ago! We were getting worried. Is everything okay?" an older man with a weather-worn baseball cap asked.

"Hey, Paul, I'm so sorry I didn't call earlier. I must have my head up my ass. Can you forgive me?" she said, adding a little extra sweet-talking to her tone.

"Well, I suppose this one time, but that's not like you to pull some stunt like that. What happened?" he asked.

"As soon as we got airborne, my entire electronic panel blew out. I decided to turn back instead of trying to make it here with no comms. I felt so bad not being able to get my passenger here on time, I chartered Tony's helicopter and caught a ride here to explain this to you myself," she lied like a pro.

"Okay, well, just as long as you're all right. You didn't have to bother flying over, you could have just called," he said.

"What?! And miss a chance to see you! No way!" she put on as thick as molasses but it worked.

She gave him a wink as we made our way out the front door, just for good measure. When we were well out of earshot it was time to get some answers.

"Okay, Jon, I give up, how did you find us," I asked with a smile.

"You must have forgotten to stop sharing your last Garmin Live Tracking session with us because we've been able to see your location for the last week, or at least where your watch has been," he began. "We got concerned when you went for a run last night so late and then when you drove to Aspen. That wasn't on the original plan but we know you make stuff up as you go sometimes so no one was overly concerned."

"We figured you were taking a plane back from Aspen, since your track and speed was too straight and fast to be a car. That's when we got concerned," he said with a quizzical look on his face.

We reached the car and all piled in. They had rented an SUV, which was perfect for the amount of people and gear that we had. We had two missions to accomplish while we were here and both took a lot of equipment. A van would have been better but the race director discouraged vehicles that large on the running course so an SUV was the next best choice. Jon put us on the road for the short drive back into town.

"You hadn't been in the plane very long and then your tracker just stopped sending data. You were around 15,000 feet at the time according to your Garmin but it never showed you descending. It just went completely dead. We knew there were some normal explanations for that but nothing you do is normal, so we immediately started to expect the worse," he continued.

"A few minutes later, something strange happened, and we were having a hard time coming up with an explanation, other than your Garmin was seriously screwed up. Your Garmin gave coordinates that you were in orbit. At first, we thought it must be reading one of the GPS satellites but then Steph started with her wild theories, which suddenly didn't sound too wild. By the time we all agreed that you probably *were* in orbit, your Garmin suddenly read you were back in a plane, but the plane was rapidly descending. Eventually, the map showed you moving again so we figured you were on foot and that's when we started making calls for transportation to pick you up," he finished.

"Yeah, that's pretty much what happened. I'll fill you in on the rest of the story when we get to the restaurant. I don't want to tell this story twice and it will sound much better after that first beer," I said.

"How did you luck out finding Tony?" I asked

"We asked around and found there was a guy who gives helicopter rides so I called and luckily he was available. Actually, he sounded pretty excited to have some business. I paid him twice his going rate if he promised to ask no questions and to keep this quiet. Then I threw in some extra for the time it took to wait for you. I told him we might use him again if our trip remains a private affair. We'll see. I think he was pretty happy in the end."

"We looked at a map and saw that open field was in line with your path so that was our best option for landing. Unfortunately, that left you a few more miles of walking but there weren't any other choices, so here we are," Jon finished.

"That was some great thinking, Jon, thanks!" I said.

"Yeah, thanks, Jon. I really wasn't looking forward to sleeping on some pine needles tonight," Sid said.

"All in a days' work on Team Jim," Jon shot back with a chuckle.

We pulled into town and parked on the street next to the restaurant. We exited the car and walked to the outdoor eating area where the rest of the team was already seated, apparently on their second or third beer by now, judging from the empty glasses on the table. I couldn't blame them. This had taken a bit longer than anyone anticipated.

"Better late than never," I said as I approached the table.

Everyone stood up and came to give me a hug. They had concerned smiles on their faces but we were all together again so we gave a collective sigh of relief as well.

"Everyone, this is Sid, she's our new teammate. Sid, this is Karen, Stephanie, and Nathan, and you already know Jon. Where's my beer?" I said with a smile.

Nathan handed me one from the table.

"It might not be as cold as the next one but you can't get one any quicker," he said laughing.

Karen handed Sid a full glass as well.

"I don't know what kind you like so you can wait to order or have this one," she said.

Sid took the glass and gave me a run for my money on who would finish theirs first. We both took our last gulps together.

"Okay, ready for round two!" I said

Nathan caught the server's eye and made a large circle with his finger, indicating another round of beer for everyone.

We all sat down, and everyone looked at me, waiting to hear the story.

"First, you guys should know that I've told Sid pretty much everything so we can speak freely in front of her," I said.

Everyone looked relieved and happy. It's hard to talk in circles and behind someone's back when they are right in front of you.

I recanted the story, starting when I realized that Steve had followed me to Leadville and finished with Jon standing in a field leaning against a helicopter.

"Holy shit!," Stephanie said. "Steve is a lizard and you went to space?!"

"Yep," I said, taking a sip of my third beer. I had already finished off my cheeseburger and fries and was thinking of ordering it all again. Nothing like being abducted, being in a plane crash and a walk through the woods to get your hunger raging.

"And Sid got her foot sawed off and a new one stitched back on?" Jon asked.

"Yep, it's brand new!" she said. "I can tell it's not the old one because this one doesn't have any nail polish on it. Does anyone have some? It looks weird having only one foot done," she said with a smile.

I was relieved at how well Sid was taking all of this in. The rest of the team had years to build up to this crazy adventure lifestyle but Sid went right into the frying pan. Maybe it was her military background that helped.

"So, what now?" Nathan asked.

"I say we pay our bill and walk across the street to the Silver Dollar Saloon. I want to get another look at that picture of Baby Doe, and have a shot of bourbon. I'm buying, who's in?" I asked.

Everyone raised their hand.

27

Patience

*O*nce you enter the workforce, your entire *life centers around it. From dawn till* dusk the men worked at the mine. Our one day off was spent at worship, giving homage to the gods who made us work the other six days of the week. I'm not sure when the seven day calendar week began but we counted our days by seven, simply because this was the cycle of work and rest. We didn't name our days like people do today. We relied on the moon and stars to tell us where we were in the year and what was coming next. It had apparently worked well up to this point so no one thought to change it.

It had taken me two years but I eventually worked hard enough to earn myself a promotion to be able to enter the mines. I still wasn't actually digging and collecting the gold but I was bringing water to those who did. I considered this a step up, since I was out of the hot sun most of the day, except when I had to fetch water at the collection point. One of the toughest jobs was collecting the water at the river and then bringing it to the mine. I hoped I was never picked for that job. That seemed to be given to those who had caused trouble in the past and were no longer allowed inside the mines.

The entrance to the mine was the oldest part. It was actually cut into the side of a hill and sloped downwards, into the ground. The opening was very elaborate, which seemed strange. It was a perfectly cut rectangle with large stones on either side and one over the top, resting on the side stones. Each stone was painted with gold. I had no idea how this was done. Then several drawings of many gods were painted on the stones. Maybe that was to remind the workers who they were working for. Why spend time making a beautiful entrance to a hole in the ground? Just another question I would seek an answer to.

The men who worked near the entrance were the older ones who had been there the longest. They were saved from the long journey into the deepest parts of the mining system. These were the people I wanted to speak with the most, since they should have the most knowledge about the mine. I decided to take my time and ask them questions in the future after they had accepted me as part of their group.

I had asked my father about the mines years ago but he had little information. He was the son of a merchant who was the son of a merchant. He had never been inside of the mine and had no close friends who had. But when I had asked to join in with the miners, he immediately allowed it. He must have known that would be my destiny, at least for a little while. While our soul journeys are never predestined, we certainly have a rough draft of what we aim to accomplish. Whether we follow the map or throw it in the trash is up to us. When it came time for souls to commit to my cause, they were chosen from those who had previously stayed on the path in earlier visits. My father was obviously a very mature soul.

I continued to work hard and make sure the bosses never had cause to correct or punish me. I also wanted the older workers to know I was doing my best to take care of them. Not only did I actually start to grow fond of several of them, but I knew they would be more willing to share information if they liked me. Honey, vinegar and bees. It's always been that way.

I had only been inside the first twenty-five yards of the mine. Up to that distance, and for as far as I could see, the walls were entirely filled with paintings. These had to be the oldest paintings, and they appeared to tell a story but I hadn't been able to figure out the meaning yet.

One day, as I was carrying the empty water jug through the tunnel, towards the entrance, one of the older men noticed my interest in the paintings.

"They are well done, don't you think so?" he asked. It was Ahmose, one of the older men I had seen in the mines. He was sitting against the wall, waiting for the next basket of rocks or gold to be brought to him. He would then carry them to the next person in the tunnel who would take them outside. It was a very efficient method.

"Yes, those who painted them were very good. Do we know who they were?" I asked, trying to make it seem like an innocent conversation and not an investigation.

"Ha!" he exclaimed. "Those have been here before my father's, father's father, and ten times over!"

"Even then, the painters were very talented," I said, sounding amazed. Truly, they were very good and to think people so long ago were talented enough to paint such elaborate pictures, especially by the light of a fire, was impressive.

"Who can read such ancient stories?" I asked, baiting the hook.

"Look no further than your eyes can see!" he said with more than a little pride.

Bait taken, now to gently reel in the catch.

"I have been looking at these for many weeks now, but they are only pictures to me. I did not dare believe there was anyone alive who was wise enough to tell me what they meant," I said, trying to sound as genuine as possible.

"My father taught me to read these and I imagine he learned the same way," he began. "These tell the story of how the god Set came to this land many lifetimes ago. Set and his lesser gods found our lands contained multitudes of gold and began collecting it. Soon, they discovered there was more gold than they were able to collect so they commanded those who worshipped them to collect the gold for them, in exchange for protection against evil gods."

"When the easily collected gold from the land and streams began to wane, they opened this hole in the mountain for us to enter and begin pulling the gold from within. The deeper we dug, the more we found, until these many years later, we have not exhausted its supply," he explained.

"You did not look at the walls as you told me this story," I pointed out to Ahmose.

"Boy, I have read this story so many times, I should have been the one to paint it myself. I have seen every bit of these walls a thousand times over, and maybe more. No one here is better than I at reading, but no one cares anymore. As long as I move the rocks from here to there is the only care they seem to have," he said, with more than a hint of bitterness in his tone.

"Do we know why our god Set wants the gold or what happens to it after he takes it?" I asked.

"Boy, do not ever ask those questions beyond these walls. If those outside heard you question the gods, then you risk your next breath," he said in a hushed tone.

"But is it safe to ask you, Ahmose?" I said, as low as I thought he might hear me.

"Truly, it is not known. Perhaps the priests know but to ask them would risk an unpleasant death. It is best to simply work and stay silent about these matters," he warned.

"Maybe you can teach me how to read these walls, so I might pass it along to my sons one day," I prompted, trying to appeal to his pride and heritage.

"Perhaps," he said. "Ask me again after we come back from our day of praising the gods. If you still show interest, I will begin to teach you."

"Thank you, Ahmose. I look forward to your wisdom," I said.

"We will see," he said.

We both returned to work, before we were missed.

28

Silver Dollar

I settled up the bill and we made a beeline across the street. The Silver Dollar Saloon is one of the true gems of The West. Built in the late 1800s, it's a living, breathing example of an era gone by. But what makes it so interesting is although it's a tourist destination, it never gave in to the tourist trap stupidity many historic spots have slid into. There are no trinkets to buy, no goofy photos with people dressed like cowboys, and no shows that pander to out-of-towners. It's a saloon. It's always been a saloon and hopefully it always stays one. If you want a drink, saddle up to the bar and order a shot.

Don't get me wrong, the place is very cool and if you catch the bartender in the right mood, she will give you a world-class history lesson about the town, the bar, and all of the colorful characters that have at one time had a drink here or called it home. Doc Holiday not only drank here but occasionally tended the bar himself. Molly Brown, of unsinkable fame, found herself on a barstool more than once. Even Oscar Wilde wet his whistle here during a tour. Walking on those floors invokes the spirits of the past.

We made our way through the authentic swinging doors and up to the bar. The same bartender was working as when I had wandered in a few days ago for a quick look around, which turned into three shots of bourbon and a dissertation on Leadville. Everyone won. I got some good bourbon and she got to practice her history lesson. It earned her a worthy tip.

"Hi, Delores, how's it going tonight?" I asked, hoping she would remember me so this would go smoothly.

"Evening. Looks like you found some friends. Whatcha having this evening?" she asked.

Despite the huge amount of visitors in town, the saloon had few people inside. Too many healthy runners afraid of libations prior to their event. The place would probably be packed the day after the race.

"Delores, can I have a bottle of your best bourbon, six glasses, and use your private room in the back?" I asked, hoping she remembered her last tip from me.

She grabbed a full bottle and six glasses and put them on the bar.

"Do ya wanna pay now or keep a tab open?" she asked.

"Let's pay now and if I need something else, I'll come up. This should hold us for a bit," I said with a smile and a wink.

We settled up quickly and I doubled the tip I gave her last time. It was a simple thing to do in order to have some privacy.

"Okay gang, before we head to the back, I want you to take a quick look at something," I said. "Have a look at this photo of Baby Doe. This saloon is named after her daughter, Rose Mary Echo Silver Dollar Tabor. Just take some notice of what appears to be a necklace with some interesting ornamental piece hanging from it. Everyone get a good glimpse? Okay, let's head to the back," I said.

We made it to the rear of the building and through a door, into a small, private room with some comfortable chairs, a table and floor lamps. I wondered what history this room may have entertained all those years ago.

I sat the glasses on the table and cracked the bottle open. This wasn't the most expensive bourbon in the world but you really wouldn't expect to find that here anyhow. However, Old Rip Van Winkle twenty-year-old Kentucky bourbon wasn't cheap, by any means. Being born in Kentucky this time around, I had a keen appreciation for the love and dedication that went into this wonderful liquid. I poured each glass and we all held them up.

"Here's to good friends," I said, and we all took a sip.

"So, you all have now seen the photo, thoughts?" I asked.

"Since you brought our attention to the necklace," Stephanie began, "I suppose there's some significance to it. It's hard to tell from that old picture, but nothing about the medallion or the necklace seemed outstanding. If it were made of silver or gold, I imagine it was very expensive."

"Anyone else," I asked, but was met with stares that told me to just go ahead and spill the beans.

"Okay, this is going to be another one of those *trust me* moments. That medallion is the exact same one worn by some interesting space friends that I have intel on. You need to have the medallion to operate their particular ship. No medallion, no making the ship go zoom," I said. "I'm hoping that the ship we've been searching for is the same one the medallion operates."

Sid was the only one who looked at me like I might be crazy, which everyone else noticed with some amusement. Then she caught herself.

"Nevermind. I was going to ask questions but after the day I've had, I just need to give in and accept whatever crazy shit comes out of your mouth," she said.

"It really works easier that way. Anyone here is welcome to tell her if any of my crazy shit hasn't panned out correctly in the past," I said.

"Nope, all of Jim's crazy shit ends up being true shit," Stephanie said laughing, and toasted her glass to me, to which I toasted back.

"A toast to crazy shit!" I said, and we all took another sip.

"So now, here is our mission while we are in Leadville. Number 1: Find out what became of that medallion. Number 2: Get me across the finish line at the race in under thirty hours. Number 3: Finish this bottle after the race," I said.

We all held up our glasses and tossed back the last bit of bourbon.

"To the bottle!" Jon toasted.

"To the bottle!" everyone replied.

29

Off Script

I knew I was stepping beyond my original assignment, but just learning to be human seemed too easy. I was a human and going about the otherwise normal, boring life of someone my age. I felt like I was wasting too much time when I could actually be learning more about the lizards and their motivations. Morah and Academ could obviously see what I was doing and so far I hadn't been given any signs to cease and desist. I wasn't even sure if they would ever contact me while I was on Earth. We had never discussed such things. I was starting a list of questions and concerns for the next time I saw them. Maybe that's what they wanted me to do all along.

For the last few months, I had met with Ahmose as often as I found time. He had slowly began teaching me the meaning of the pictures on the wall. They were not entirely different from those that people painted in our time but just dissimilar enough to make the meanings change with just one mistaken decipher. By the end of our lessons, Ahmose declared that I had learned all he could teach and to leave him be. I had probably worn the old man out with my questions so it was just as well that school was over.

I had read and reread the stories over and over, trying to find some clue as to why the visitors wanted gold and why they had turned us into grateful slaves to work for them. Finally, it dawned on me the common thread that I had been overlooking. The priests. During every encounter with the lizard gods, the priests were their envoys. The gods would never speak one-on-one with a lowly common human but the priests seemed to have their ear to some extent.

If I wanted to get closer to the lizards, I needed to get closer to the priests. This was a challenge that I felt very excited about. I was making my own plans on how to plot against the lizards. It felt good to have some specific goal and direction now. I needed a new plan.

The next day was for giving praise to our god. The priests led most of the proceedings for such days. They would tell us why we should be grateful to be under the watch of Set and how we could never do enough to justify his protection from the other evil gods. Our only way to repay his gift was to work harder to supply him with gold. I had heard these lectures for all my life but now they took on more of a nefarious tone.

However, during this proceeding, I watched the priests more closely. To help them with their many extra chores of moving items around or keeping food and drink close by, they used several young men, not much older than I was. The priests would never lift an item themselves or appear in any way to take part in some menial task that required effort. Instead, the boys would be close by to do any task that was called upon. Everyone seemed to know where to be and when to be there, as if it were a rehearsed dance. Looking at it from this point of view made it all much more interesting.

I needed to find out how to become one of the servants to the priests. I had no idea how these boys were picked. Information was needed. I would start with my father first. Family could be trusted with these delicate topics and any help needed to move my mission forward. Time to change my career path.

30

Who's Who

There was only so much we could talk about sitting around a table in a public place, even one as seemingly private as this back room. It was time to move this party to the house. It was only a few blocks away and we could have easily walked but Jon had the car so we all piled in for the short drive. He had conspicuously drank less than everyone else so he had named himself designated driver. We headed for the door.

"Can I borrow someone's phone?" Sid asked. "I better check in to let my friends know I won't be returning to Aspen soon. They'll send out a search party if I go missing and I imagine we don't like to draw that kind of attention to what's going on. Am I correct?"

"Correct," I said as Karen handed her a phone.

"Hi, Craig," we heard Sid begin her phone call. "I decided not to come back to Aspen for a little while................no, everything is okay...............I just decided to take a little R & R. Can you do me a favor?...........Can you run by the hangar and make sure to lock everything up for me. I'll be back in a few days..............Thanks, Craig, tell everyone I'll see them soon." She handed the phone back to Karen.

"Those guys are a bunch of worrywarts and if I hadn't shown back up soon, they would all be out looking for me and making calls to every police department from here to Arkansas," she said. "We all take care of each other out there. I don't have much family left, so they kind of adopted me when I showed up a few years ago."

"Family is good," Stephanie said. "It's good someone has your back." Everyone looked at each other and nodded in agreement. We knew about having each other's back.

We pulled up to the rental house. Actually, we only rented the second story of the house. The ground floor was occupied by the owners. They were a sweet older couple who had bought and rehabbed the building decades ago but it was much too large for just the two of them. When their kids moved away, they turned the upstairs rooms into apartments. Each room was an efficiency apartment with a shared bathroom in the hallway. It was all very cozy, as the owners had taken meticulous care to restore the house to its former glory from the 1800s. The entire floor was ours because I wanted to give the team some privacy. I thought we would have too much room to ourselves but with the addition of our new team member, we had just the right amount of beds.

We filed out of the car and marched up the wooden stairs to the front porch. Mrs. Henderson, the owner, opened the door before I had a chance to grab the doorknob.

"Looks like your crew has arrived," she said, looking everyone over, probably making sure she didn't just rent her house to a bunch of party animals.

Apparently satisfied, she said, "So, it takes all of you just to make sure one guy can run 100 miles?" she asked with a shake of her head.

"I'm a special case Mrs. Henderson but if anyone can get me across that line, these guys can," I chimed in.

"Well, good luck to the lot of you. From what I can tell you might have good weather but things change fast at this altitude," she warned.

"As long as it doesn't snow, I think we're ready for anything," I added.

"Okay, if you need more towels or sheets, just let us know," she said before disappearing back into her section on the first floor.

The house had very high ceilings and that meant the staircase going to the second floor was an extra several steps as well. By the time we hit the top floor, I could hear everyone panting a bit harder than normal. Since the team had only been here a few hours, they hadn't had time to acclimate to the elevation, and breathing the thinner air would take some time to adjust to.

"Sid, between the five of us, I'm sure we can find you something else to wear until we can do some shopping tomorrow. And we have enough toiletries to keep an army clean for a month. I'm sure you want a shower after the day you've had," Karen said after she had caught her breath.

"Karen, you read my mind or I must smell bad," Sid said with a smile.

Karen, Stephanie and Sid huddled around their luggage and put together a handful of supplies, including some clothes to borrow. After an abduction, a plane crash and a long wilderness hike, Sid's clothes had seen better days. I'm sure she was ready to get out of them and into something clean.

"When everyone has cleaned up, let's circle back to my room and have a pow wow," I said. "We need to fill in some gaps and get our plan in order."

And with that, everyone hustled around, stashing away equipment, putting suitcases away, and setting up the rest of our rooms. Everyone took their turn in the bathroom and less than an hour later, we were all back in my living room. It was a bit cramped but no one minded sitting on whatever they could find.

"Okay, let's start with who is who. You know everyone's name but you should know what each person's team responsibility is," I said.

"I guess the best way to do this is for everyone to take their turn and tell Sid why you're on the team and what you do. Sound good?" I asked, looking around. "Karen, why don't you start?"

"Sure, why not? If you haven't figured it out by now, I'm married to Jon. Jim recruited us about fifteen years ago. Our kids went to the same school so one day during our sons' baseball game, Jim struck up a conversation. At the time, I didn't realize he was giving me a recruitment test. A few weeks later, he asked us out to dinner. We met at a restaurant with private booths and that's where he laid out his plan for us to join his team for this mission. After a few questions, we joined up and the rest is history," she said, holding up her beer and then taking a swig.

"My team job is logistics. He has me doing all kinds of different shit, like the rest of the team, but logistics is my unofficial title. We go to lots of places and Jim has lots of properties around the world so I make sure we all get where we're going and all of the properties are taken care of. I think I need a staff of ten other people but I'm told that's not going to happen so I stay pretty busy," she said, giving me a bit of the evil eye.

"Jon?" I said.

"I'm Jon and I do whatever Karen tells me to do," he said with a big smile.

"If you know what's good for you," Karen said with a laugh.

"But I'm also a doctor in the real world and that's my job for the team. We end up in some weird places around the world so I make sure we're ready to go. If someone bleeds, I make it stop. If someone sneezed, I hand them a tissue," he said. Being a smart-ass was obviously a crucial criteria for being on this team.

"Steph, you're up," I said.

"I'm Stephanie, and I'm not married to Jon," she began, keeping the theme rolling.

"The outside world thinks I'm a super mom, amazing runner and a science teacher. As Jim's slave, I mean team member, I'm in charge of research. As the others have stated, Jim has us going to some pretty weird places in our quest. I track down things he needs and find the best ways to handle the local environment, wherever that may take us. It certainly keeps me hopping!" she said, also raising her beer bottle and taking a swig. "Jim found me because I'm related to Karen or at least that's the way it seemed at the time. I joined up shortly after Jon and Karen."

"Okay, Nathan, that leaves you," I said.

"I've only been on the team for about ten years," he started. "I'm an engineer on the outside and for the team. If something needs to be made, fixed, created, or turned into something else, I'm the Macgyver of the team, although Jon is pretty good at filling in when I need another set of hands," he toasted Jon.

189

"I'm related to Stephanie, so you can see the pattern here. Maybe you're related to Stephanie or Karen too. Has anyone asked her yet?" he laughed.

Sid looked back and forth between the two women and everyone laughed.

"I guess we'll find out. Sid, want to fill us in on who you are and what you bring to the team?" I said.

"I guess we'll give whole life stories later but here are the relevant parts," she began.

"I was in the Air Force as a pilot. I've flown several aircraft but my last assignment was with an F-22 Raptor squadron. I've been out for a couple of years now and decided to chill out and have some fun for a while. I bought a great little aircraft and opened up an airplane for hire business. It was a fun and easy gig and I was able to keep my toe in the flying pool."

"Recently, some weird guy wearing running clothes offered me a load of money to take him on a short flight to Leadville. During our hop, I was abducted, had my foot cut off, crashed my plane and took an unwanted hike in the woods. Now I have no plane, no business, and a new team," she said with a smile that didn't seem entirely a smile.

"So, I'm good flying stuff, have great organizational skills, and can grill a steak like nobody's business. I also dabble in making my

190

own beer, of which my latest batch will need to be bottled in the next few days, just FYI."

"Sid, you said the magic words! Beer! The rest of that stuff is okay, but the beer-making skills got you a slot on the team immediately! You should have opened with that," I said with a laugh.

"Looks like someone else can cover the flight duties now and I can concentrate on mission stuff a bit more," I said. "Although I never get tired of bussing us around on one of the jets, it does take away from other stuff now and then. Plus, having two pilots will make this much easier on everyone. Sid, if you love to fly, then you'll be a busy woman for as long as you stay with this team. You are welcome to call it quits anytime as well, and like I said, I'll replace your plane with anything you can find that's for sale. You just say what and when, and I'll make sure it's yours. Sound good?" I finished.

She looked around the room, seeing if that sounded like bullshit to anyone else, but everyone just waited for her answer.

"Deal," she said.

"Okay, after what I've seen so far, we need to start focusing on some new directions," I said.

"Stephanie, I need you to find out what happened to that necklace. Things will go much easier down the road if we have that in our possession," I said.

"Jon, Sid and I will get with you concerning that medical table that can apparently restore feet and bring aliens back to life. We may need some of that tech in the future. Maybe between you and Nathan, we can come up with our own working version."

"Karen, give Stephanie a hand with her mission. When we find out where that necklace is, we need to make some moves that puts us in its vicinity for a good reason."

"Sid, for now, tie up any of your own loose ends in Aspen. You'll be able to come back now and then if necessary but we have a good deal of traveling and learning for you to get caught up on. Make sure to pay special attention to getting that beer bottled before we leave town. If you need help, I'm sure I can find you some," I said, to which everyone raised their hand with a smile.

One last toast and we called it a day.

31

The Chosen Few

*A*s luck would have it, my father had been a *childhood friend of one of the* priests. Not until they were my age did their lives take different paths. My father, of course, followed in his father's profession. His friend, Rahotep, showed an aptitude towards service to the gods and became a servant to the priests and eventually a priest himself. While Rahotep and my father did not remain close, they acknowledged one another when the occasion presented itself.

When I asked my father if he might speak to his friend in order for me to become a servant to the priests, he simply said he would. No questions. No lectures. He knew that I had my own path and it was his job to help me pursue it. If I made mistakes, then they were mine alone, and I would fix them in this life or the next.

Several days later, I began to wonder if Father had seen his friend, but when I came home I found Rahotep sitting next to my father in our home. I knew his face, as I had seen him nearly every week for the last several years during our mandatory gatherings to praise Set. He was a tall man, thin, and wore the robes of a priest. Very clean. I was still dirty from working in the mines and wasn't sure this would make a good first impression.

"Sabaf, come and meet my old friend, Rahotep. Rahotep, this is my son, Sabaf," Father said.

"Please excuse my clothing, sir. I have been working in the mines. I will clean myself if you give me but a few moments," I said.

"There is no need for that, Sabaf," he said. "It is good to see a boy who is not afraid of work. Wear your dirt proudly. Your father tells me you have an interest in becoming a priest's servant. Why is that?" he asked.

"I am trying to serve the gods as best I can in this life. I am working in the mines to show them my devotion. As I attended one of our day of thanks to the gods, I was struck with the idea that I might better serve the gods by assisting their priests and, with the blessings of the priests and gods, one day become a priest myself," I said with as much conviction as I could.

"Could it be that you tire of the hard work of the mines and simply wish a job with less labor?" he asked with raised eyebrows.

"Oh no! I would work in the mines until my dying day if that is where the gods believed I would best serve. I simply felt a special call within my bones as we all gave thanks to our gods. Perhaps everyone feels this special summons as the priests guide us through the ceremonies. I knew I must at least pursue this call, and allow a higher power to decide my path," I said.

He took a step back and looked me up and down and then once again. He crossed his arms over his chest and closed his eyes, as if in deep thought. We all stood still. Waiting. Did he fall asleep standing up? Was that possible? Finally, he opened his eyes and smiled.

"The gods believe your path would be better served by assisting the priests. But be warned, this is not an easy task. You will start before the sun rises, and many days come home well after it departs. You must learn quickly and never bring disgrace to yourself, the priests, your family, or the gods. Do you believe you can perform such a service?" he asked.

Not wanting to seem as if I did not consider his words, I did not answer immediately. I waited a few seconds, as if giving his words the proper respect that he meant them with.

"It would give me great honor to assist you and the other priests in the service of our gods. I will bring honor to you, my family and our people if given this chance," I said, hoping I sounded and looked convincing.

"Then clean yourself and rest. I will see you at the Temple of the Priests as the light precedes the sun," he said.

"Thank you," I said, and left to wash as father and Rahotep spoke together.

My plan seemed to be proceeding. I hoped
Morah and Academ approved.

32

Prep

The next morning we got an early start. There were things to do. Sid, Jon, Nathan and I decided to become tourists and head up to the Matchless Mine. Baby Doe stood by that site to the very end despite knowing it was a loser of a mine so something had to inspire her. Maybe there were some Scooby Doo clues we could turn up.

Stephanie headed back to the saloon to see if there were any leads on where that necklace may have gone. The owner and the bartender seemed well steeped in the history of the town and all of its colorful past. Maybe there was a story about the necklace too.

Karen stayed behind to organize the upcoming race. People had their parts to do to make sure this event went smoothly and Karen was a master of logistics. Telling people where to go and what to do in the right tone to motivate them was a gift and she had it in spades. It's nice to have a well oiled machine of a team. I hoped I didn't need to assemble another team in the next life because it would be hard to surpass this one. Time would tell.

The Matchless Mine was only a ten-minute ride up a dirt road, just east of the town. We parked in the small lot, next to a tiny wooden building that seemed to be the office. Apparently, this wasn't as popular a tourist destination as some might hope for. We were the only people there. I suppose the runners had other priorities. Or maybe they just weren't trying to find alien technology.

The four of us got out of the SUV and walked up to the office as a middle-aged man in a ranger outfit exited.

"Good morning," Robert said. We knew it was Robert because of the name tag displayed on his shirt. "Have you come to take the tour?" he asked.

"We sure have," I said. "Are we your first customers today?"

"Yes, sir, and judging from the number of people we had yesterday, you may be the only ones to visit all day," he said with a glum expression. "The tour is self-guided. There are plaques stationed at different areas explaining what you are seeing and the history of the area. Just stay on the path and enjoy the tour. If you have any questions, feel free to ask before you leave. That will be $10 per person."

I pulled out a couple of twenties and handed them to Robert.

"Thank you, sir," I said and we proceeded towards the first plaque which gave a brief history of how mining came to Leadville and the different ores that were produced and how things have changed over the years. There were plenty of reminders of the past all around us. It seemed that the miners never really cared what they destroyed or about the leftover machines and tools they no longer needed. They simply threw or dragged equipment just as far as needed so they didn't trip over it. The hillsides were littered with rusted pieces of odd metal that defied description.

We moved from plaque to plaque until we stood in front of the tiny shack next to the shaft that lead into the last working mine. This is where Baby Doe had lived for decades and this is where they found her dead one morning when nearby residents noticed no smoke coming from her chimney. This plaque told of the rise and demise of Elizabeth McCourt Tabor, better known as Baby Doe.

The legends written allege her late husband, Horace, told her to hold on to the mine with his dying breath because someday the mine would produce again. I had my suspicions as to this story and believed there was another reason. One that had nothing to do with silver or any other types of ore. I believed the Matchless Mine held a secret.

After walking through her one-room clapboard house, we exited and stood around the long-closed entrance to the mine. This wasn't the traditional mine that one might think of. It was a hole in the ground that descended straight down. According to the mock-up model of the mine in the building next door, there were several levels of tunnels below us. We needed to take a look.

I had an idea that self-guided tours of the tunnels were frowned upon since there was a locked door to the entrance as well as a sign that declared the area was off limits. This seemed like a good time to ask Ranger Robert for some information.

"That was a quick tour. Do you have any questions?" he asked with a big smile on his face.

"As a matter of fact, Robert, I'd like to know if we can go down into the mine," I said, with an equally big smile.

He just started laughing, as if I was telling the best joke he had heard in a long time, but when we didn't all join in on the laughing, he abruptly stopped.

"Well, uh, no sir. No one is allowed in the mine anymore. It's too dangerous. Many of the tunnels have collapsed over the years and it's been ages since anyone has even opened the hatch to the tunnel," he said with a concerned look on his face.

"Wow!" I said. "That's a shame. It would have been really cool to see what the miners had to go through to bring that ore out of the ground," I said.

"That mock-up of the tunnels was made while the mines were still in use so it's a pretty good example of what things were like back then," he said.

"Yeah, but nothing like standing in the actual tunnel, I bet," I said.

"There are some other mines you can tour in the area if you're interested," he said, trying to console us. I'm sure he got that question enough that he had a quick answer.

"That's okay. We're kind of busy the rest of the trip but we'll mention it to other runners and maybe we can drum up some business for you," I said as we began walking back to the car.

"Thanks a lot!" he yelled back.

We all climbed back into the car, Jon in the driver's seat.

"We're coming back here tonight and busting into that mine, aren't we?" Jon asked with a smile on his face.

"Jon, you know me well," I smiled back.

33

I Spy

*O*ver the next several years I played the part of a dutiful servant to the priests. I came early and stayed late, always volunteering for any extra job that needed to be done, no matter how menial. The priests needed to believe that I was the most devout servant in their flock. I needed their absolute trust for when the lizards made their next appearance.

As the date of Set's next visit drew near, things in the community began to ramp up. The streets were cleaned more often. Gold production increased, even beyond its already previous breakneck schedule. The priests began final preparations for the gods arrival. If a thing could shine, it needed to sparkle. If a piece of cloth had a tear, it was repaired or replaced. Each servant was assigned a duty to perform, and we were to practice over and over until we could do it blindfolded.

As one of the oldest and best-trained servants, I had worked my way into the inner circle of the priests. They believed I would soon enter the priesthood so they would occasionally show me some of their duties and what would be expected of me once I took the special vows.

I had one specific job in mind for the arrival of Set and his cohorts. As the gold was being loaded into their ship, the gods and the priests would have a small banquet together to rejoice. It was during this time the gods would give their expectations for their next arrival, which usually consisted of warnings if there wasn't even more gold the next time they arrived. During this banquet, there would be two servants needed to bring food and drink or fetch any of the many ceremonial objects that were waved around while chanting.

Only the most trusted and mature servants were given this job and it was no accident I positioned myself to be one of those servants. In fact, being the highest ranking servant, it was my task to pick one other helper to assist in this most coveted appointment.

Over the last few years, I began to groom a fellow servant, Theshen, to be my trusted friend. I made sure he was better trained than the others and that he showed the appropriate degree of enthusiasm for the job when it mattered most. I wanted to make sure he would have the easy approval of the priests when it came time to choose my assistant for the banquet. Although he was nearly two years younger than I was, he stood out nearly as much as I did among other servants. Theshen trusted me completely and that was exactly what I would need when the time came.

My plan was simple. Stay as close as possible to the gods after they arrived. I wanted to learn as much as possible from them as I could. As this was my first time being near them as a human, I would be in an interesting position to observe them. I only hoped all of these years of preparation wasn't a waste. I had done everything I could think of to make this mission successful. Now all I could do was wait and take advantage of opportunities when they presented themselves. Learning and acting swiftly was a skill, and although it came with a degree of danger, I only became more excited. As long as my true identity and

plan was never discovered, I had nothing to lose and everything to gain.

And then one evening, comet Set made its appearance in the night sky. Everyone had been scanning the heavens for days, waiting to catch the first glimpse of the coming god. Tomorrow morning, for the first time in nearly eight years, the gods would be among us once again. I was as ready as I could be. Now all I can do is wait.

34

Breadcrumbs

That night for dinner, we met back at the Tennessee Pass Café. I had called ahead to rent out the entire back room and requested the head waitress as our personal server, securing her and the room with a sizable retainer. I made mention that the pot would be sweetened if we could depend on privacy and was assured we would not be disturbed. The owner knew the value of high spenders and repeat customers so we spoke the same language. Some things never change and they shouldn't.

After we were all seated and ordered our food, it was time to see what Stephanie had learned. She had hinted that she had a doozy of a story but refused to tell a word of it until someone put a plate of food in front of her. Food on the way, it was time to spill the beans.

"Okay, Steph, give us the scoop. What did you find out today?" I asked.

"You're gonna love this!" she said. "I'm sure by now you know the story of poor Baby Doe, since you visited the mines this morning. After being one of the wealthiest people in the United States, she became penniless, and ended up dying in that shack you saw today. Doe's story is interesting but the necklace has its own tale. Horace, her husband, gave the necklace to Elizabeth during the height of their wealth, when the mines were producing and seemed to possess an unending supply of silver. What we don't know is where the necklace came from. He never mentions buying it so its origins remain a mystery but what we do know is pretty cool. When Baby Doe lost everything and her husband had died, her long time Leadville friend, Meyer Guggenheim, offered to buy the necklace from her so she would have money to eat. Meyer is the first of the Guggenheims to be wealthy and it all started with the mines in Leadville. Meyer, Baby Doe and Horace all traveled in the same social circles for years since they all struck it rich here. Anyhow, Baby Doe was reluctant to sell the necklace, since it was the last thing she had from her late husband but apparently she had little choice. Meyer bought the necklace and Baby Doe was able to live off that sale until her dying day," she said.

At that point, the food arrived and we waited until everyone had a plate in front of them and a fresh drink. Then she proceeded with the story.

"Okay, so, Meyer was pretty old by this point and died the very next year. Meyer had a slew of children but somehow his middle son, Benjamin, ends up with the necklace. Now, believe it or not, all of you know who Benjamin Guggenheim is because I'm sure all of you have seen the movie *Titanic*. Ben was the lucky Guggenheim to score a first-class ticket on this historic crossing. But the good news is that before getting on the boat, he gave his twelve-year-old daughter, Peggy, a very special gift. Any guesses?" she said with a sly smile.

"So," she continued, "that was of course in April, 1912 and we all know what happened to poor Ben and it wasn't running around with Rose or Jack. Fortunately, Peggy's life is well documented and in 1920, she decided to take a job in a bookstore in New York. The bookstore was called The Sunwise Turn, and was partially owned by Harold Loeb, who was also related to the Guggenheims, meaning Harold was Peggy's cousin. She, of course, didn't need the job, but she felt she needed to see what a job felt like and the store was kind of the epicenter of coolness at the time. Anybody who was anybody in the literary world made their way to this bookstore to just hang out and talk and have coffee."

"One of those anybodies was a ruggedly handsome guy named Ernest Hemmingway, also the same age as Peggy, and a great lover of women. It didn't take long before these two hooked up and had a summer fling that by all accounts was pretty hot and heavy."

"Unfortunately, or maybe fortunately for us, the romance came to an end when Peggy moved to Paris at the end of that year. But before she left, she wanted to give Ernest a memento to remember her by. Yup! You guessed it! The necklace!" she said with mock surprise.

"Apparently Ernest pined for her until his dying day and kept the necklace very close to him, no matter who he happened to be married to at the time. So, that's the story of the necklace," she finished.

"Uh, I don't think so," I said, knowing she had one last bit to tell. "You forgot the most important part."

"Oh,yeah. You have to run another 100 mile race after this one," she said with a toothy smile and a wink.

"Shit! I haven't even run *this* one yet and you already want me to run another one?" I complained.

"Yup, 'cause that necklace is sitting in Key West, inside Ernest Hemmingway's house, on a shelf, across from his bed. It was the last thing he would see every night and the first thing he would see every morning. Isn't that romantic?" she said, adding a dreamy lilt to her voice.

"I'm guessing our cover will be doing the Keys 100 Ultra Marathon?" I asked.

"Bingo!" she said, taking a big swig of the cold beer in front of her.

"Key West, here we come," I said as I raised my glass in a toast.

"Key West!" we said.

35

Rut Row

*J*ust as before, Set and his fellow lesser gods did not disappoint. They came blasting across the sky in a very flamboyant display of their power and might. For those who were new to the spectacle, there was no doubt about all of the stories they had heard. When you see a giant shiny object hurling itself through the air, so close you feel like you might touch it, you became an absolute believer. Now it was time to put my new position to use.

As the ship began to land, Theshen and I rushed inside the temple to await the priests, Set, and his entourage. They would gather here for a feast, and to discuss the day's events and their expectations for the future. This time, Theshen and I would be present while fetching food and drink. I was ready.

My heart was racing and I could feel my palms sweating as the priests lead the way through the door and into the banquet area. Theshen and I had the large rectangular table set with our finest wares, ready to serve the wine and figs before the main plates came out. Several goats had been prepared for the feast and would come later. No item had been spared which could possibly be offered. We would deny them nothing. Set himself came through the door, after our priests and ahead of his lesser god buddies. He was such an odd creature to behold, regardless of knowing what he actually was. Each of the lizards had taken a frightening form to produce the god effect and it certainly worked. After they entered the room, they all stood in their places around the table. Set sat down, then the lesser gods sat, then the priests sat. Theshen and I began serving the gods our best wine, starting with Set.

I stood right next to him as I poured the wine. All the while, I was trying to look at Set without appearing to stare. As I poured, he spoke to the god "lizard" to his right.

"I dread this part most of all, Drubis," Set said. He was speaking the language of the lizards, which the priests could not understand. Thankfully, I had been gifted with the ability to understand all languages so my job was made a bit easier. I only had to pretend not to know what was being discussed.

"This is the foulest beverage in all the galaxy! Thank Stumus we don't come to this lump of a world very often. Enduring their food is enough to test the guts of any Draconian!" he spat towards his friend.

"Yes, but they do provide a certain entertainment from time to time when the urge strikes," he laughed as he seemed to think he just told the best joke ever spoken.

Unfortunately, it was this "joke" that was taking a toll on the human population. Set and his friends seemed to use **Earth** as their private party outpost and creating hybrid humans was not good for the human or the soul who could no longer merge with that being. Then as those hybrids had offspring, the foulness was passed along as those babies could not hold a soul. If left unchecked, this would destroy the race sooner than later.

The priests were deathly quiet while Set spoke. No one dared to speak to him unless he asked a question first.

"Gretimus, how do you plan to stop these humans from their rapid self-advancement?" Drubis asked Set, whose real name was apparently Gretimus.

Gretimus? I knew that name. He was the Draconian who was supposed to make sure Crumbius finished his mission. It appeared that Crumbius was out of the picture, probably dead, and Gretimus was now in charge. It was Earth they were discussing when Morah took me to Draconia to learn about the lizards. I needed to think about all of this but not at this moment.

"I have a genius plan I will discuss with you later," he said. "For now, let's move through these proceedings as quickly as possible and leave this wretched rock," Gretumus/Set said.

"Agreed," said Drubis.

Theshen and I continued to serve at the appropriate times, just as we had been taught to do. The main course was served and every known food available was put before the gods. The average Egyptian would have been astounded at the mounds of food on the table, most of which was going uneaten. The gods themselves were barely eating anything and Set ate nothing at all. Perhaps they wanted to give the impression that gods did not need such trivial things as food to keep them alive.

Eventually, the foods were finished being served and Set began to congratulate the priests on the goals being met from the previous visit and to once again set the bar even higher for the next one. It was during this conversation that I put my plan into action. I pulled Theshen aside and spoke with him in a low tone.

"Theshen, you will need to see to the needs of the ceremony by yourself for a short period while I locate a fresh cask of beer," I lied.

"Sabaf!" he exclaimed. "I can not do this without you!"

"Theshen, we have practiced this a thousand times together. You can do this blindfolded. The ceremony is nearly finished and Set wants to take a cask of beer as he leaves. I must find a fresh one immediately. You will be fine. Now go and do not worry," I said.

As soon as Theshen left me, I exited the building and walked straight to Set's ship. It had been left completely unattended, as everyone was either inside the great hall or gathered around it waiting to see the great procession when it emerged. I took one last glance to make sure I had no eyes looking in my direction and walked quickly up the ramp leading into the ship.

Once inside, the godlike perceptions began to fade, at least in my estimation. While clearly advanced, it became apparent that the gods needed very normal devices to move about the heavens. Pipes of various sizes were routed this way and that. The floor was just a floor, made from different elements than were available to Egyptians but it was just a floor. There were colors of every different kind on different items or areas but none of it looked to be made from the gold we were supplying them in vast quantities. It simply looked alien, not godlike, but I'm sure alien and godlike could be used interchangeably if you didn't know any better. The room I was in was about the size of the banquet hall, and was completely filled with all of the gold we had mined over the last several years. It must have been loaded while I was inside serving the feast. If anyone entered, I would be easily seen. I needed to get out of this room.

Once my eyes adjusted to the interior, I saw several doors but there was just no way to tell where they led to. I really didn't even know what I was looking for. I was on a fishing expedition, just hoping to turn up anything to help me later when I had more skills.

Not wanting to be seen, I ran across the room and took the door to the furthest right which led to a passage. The passage began to show signs of other doorways on the left and right sides but they were all closed, with no apparent way to open them. I had gone much further than I felt comfortable when I decided I should go back outside. I was finding nothing useful and being discovered would only jeopardize the lives of my people. I turned around and started back towards the main room I entered.

When I reached the end of the passage and was about to enter the room with the exit, I could hear people coming up the ramp. No! Not now! I only needed another moment. I pushed myself back a short distance into the passage, so as not to be seen but close enough I might hear what they said.

"Okay, crew, feel free to change back into your true form when in suits you," Gretimus said. "We leave immediately. Control, once we are in the air, make several impressive godlike passes over the fools on the ground. Let's give them a show. Fly high enough to not kill anyone but low enough to almost kill everyone!" he said with a laugh.

"Everyone meet me in the eating hall and we will discuss my plan for this planet. I'm famished. I was not going to insult my body with their crude offerings. Do not be late. It is time we begin to take control of this rock. Stumus will kill us all if our results are not better than those of my predecessor," he hissed.

I peeked around the door only to witness the ramp to the outside was closing. Almost immediately, I felt my stomach lurch and I knew that the ship had left the ground. With me inside. This was not part of my plan. I needed to make better plans.

36

Miner 49er

I didn't have to pack all of the gear needed to pull off our next adventure. All of the towns in this part of the country usually had a well supplied outdoor shop and Leadville was no exception. Ropes, flashlights, helmets, gloves, everything a group of people needed to break into and explore long abandoned silver mines.

We had picked up all of our supplies after dinner and took it back to the house to set up our packs. Jon, Nathan, and I each had a small backpack which we filled with what we hoped were the proper items needed to pull this off. I had been spelunking a few times in the past and this probably wasn't much different. At least that's what I told myself.

We waited until an hour after dark before we left the house. Karen and Sid drove us to the dirt road where the Matchless Mine was located and dropped us about a half mile from its entrance. The road was completely deserted since the only destinations on these roads were the mines. By all accounts, if anyone did happen to pass by us, we simply looked like hikers, of which there was a never ending abundance of in these parts. I couldn't imagine anyone else driving out here unless they were some teenagers looking for a spot to drink or have a romantic rendezvous. Or perhaps a runner looking to kill a lizard posing as a nosy investigator. But that was pretty outlandish.

Sunrise would be at 6:19am so we needed to be finished and out of here well before then. We told Karen and Sid to meet us at our pick up point at 5am. That should give us enough time to find anything that might be helpful. Should. We were completely playing this by the seat of our pants, which we were all more than comfortable doing. However, a solid plan is usually a more productive way to go.

The moon was only a quarter illuminated but high in the night sky. It provided just a hint of light so we didn't need to use our flashlights or head lamps. No need to give our location away. You could see these headlamps for miles. Stealth is your friend.

Ten minutes later we were at the entrance to the mine. What a sad and lonely place for Baby Doe to live like a hermit all of those years. Even now, it was desolate. Elizabeth had the miners for company for several years as she lived her. But after the mine closed, she was here all alone. For a very long time. If she wanted supplies or conversation, she had a long walk back into town. However, I knew in the back of my mind that she had picked this journey for herself for her own reasons so I didn't really feel sorry for her. Sometimes, even now, it was easy to get caught up in the emotions of the human experience and forget the soul is on its own path.

We paused at the gate next to the little house that sat at the entrance to the mine. We had scouted the place for cameras or motion detectors earlier and found none but we still did a quick double check to make sure we didn't miss anything. Truthfully, this little tourist mine seemed a bit strapped for cash and although the ranger we met put on a good face, the place seemed as abandoned as ever. Not much to steal, not much to destroy. Pouring money into a security system for this place must have felt unnecessary and a bad use of already thin resources. I felt pretty confident we were very alone here tonight.

We walked the thirty yards to Baby Doe's shack of a house, which stood next to the covered and locked entrance to the mine. We stood around the metal door that had been fashioned over the hole to discourage people from climbing down into the mine. With only a small, simple lock holding the door secure, Nathan extracted his bolt cutter from his pack and snipped the lock free with one easy squeeze of the handles. He grabbed the pieces of the lock and threw them over the ridge. They would mix with the other million pieces of old mining equipment dumped here for decades, never to be found again.

Jon and I grabbed opposite sides of the door and began to lift it on its hinges, only to be met with a loud squeak that sounded like a jet engine blasting down the runway. We stopped immediately and looked at each other. It sounded like this could be heard a mile away.

"Anyone bring some WD-40?" I asked, already knowing the answer.

"Let's just tear off this band-aid and do it quick," Nathan said. "I really doubt there is anyone within earshot to hear this."

"Okay," I said. "Jon, on three. One......two......and three," and we lifted it quickly until it was completely open. The squeak was crazy loud but Nathan was right, no one would hear this and even if someone did, the echo from the hills would make it practically impossible to pinpoint the source.

I pulled my small LED flashlight from my pack and pointed it down the exposed hole. An old wooden ladder descended into the inky blackness that my light no longer reached. I looked back and forth to Nathan and Jon and they both seemed equally creeped out.

"That ladder looks like it's about to disintegrate into dust," Jon said.

"Man, do they actually still use that thing, or is it some kind of prop to discourage people like us?" I asked to no one.

"One thing's for sure. It's not going to support any of our weight. We need another ladder or a Plan B," Nathan said.

"Okay, let's split up for a minute and check the vicinity. If we see a ladder or a Plan B, we'll use it. If not, we'll move on to Plan C," I said.

"What's Plan C?" Jon asked.

"I don't know yet but when we meet back up, I'll have one," I smiled.

I took off towards the building that held the mockup cross section of the mine. It was the closest thing they had to a museum on the site so maybe I could find something useful there. Unfortunately, the building itself was locked and my quick walk around didn't produce anything. For as cluttered of a site as this one appeared at first glance, there was apparently some actual order here too. I started back empty-handed.

Nathan was back next, hands empty. Jon was only seconds behind him.

"Ok, ready for Plan C," Jon said with a smile.

"Right," I said. "Here's the plan. We make leg harnesses with our ropes and slowly lower ourselves into the mine, using the relic of a ladder as a guide, but putting little to no weight on it if we can help it."

They just stared at me.

"Hey, I didn't say Plan C was going to be awesome, I just said it was a plan," I said.

"Want to show us this leg harness?" Nathan asked with a bit of healthy skepticism.

"Several years ago, I did a little stint as a firefighter. We used a rope to tie a leg harness to extract ourselves from high places as a last resort. It's an easy harness to tie but not one you'd use unless you didn't have access to a normal harness. It will be fine for what we need tonight. Coming up will be a bit less fun, but our options are limited," I explained.

"Okay, grab your rope and do what I do," I said.

They each pulled their ropes from their packs and I slowly began twisting and tying the rope until it was fashioned into an acceptable, lifesaving harness. I did it slowly enough they were each able to follow my example. While it wasn't as pretty as a fancy store bought harness, it would do the job. From the looks of the model earlier, we had about thirty feet to descend, which was good because we each only had forty feet of rope and about six of that was used to tie the harness.

"Okay, this is my mission so I'll go first," I said.

They both looked at each other and then at me with a bit of relief on their faces. It was just a hole in the ground. Just because the rangers had mentioned cave-ins and lack of air didn't mean this might be dangerous.

I hitched the end of the rope around a rusty pipe next to the opening and positioned myself to go down.

"Last one down is a rotten egg," I smiled, and took the first step into the hole. I put my right foot on the very outside portion of the second rung, not wanting to test the middle. Somehow, it didn't snap like a toothpick. I put my left foot on the next rung, trying to keep as much of my weight on the rope and off the ladder as possible.

"Okay, I'll let you know when I'm at the bottom. Hopefully, I'll get there before I run out of rope," I said.

I kept lowering myself down. As soon as my head was below the ground, everything changed. I could smell the rock and dirt from the shaft and tunnels below me. Not being claustrophobic, there was certainly a sense of being closed in, as the shaft itself was only four feet across, at most. Slowly, step by step, I made my way down. The air took on a life of its own life as the temperature began to drop and I could feel the pressure in my ears changing, which seemed strange for only going fifteen or twenty feet down so far. The ladder hadn't collapsed yet, a good sign, but I still didn't dare put one more ounce on it than absolutely necessary, no matter how much the rope was beginning to dig into the backs of my legs. I only had about ten more feet to go. Hopefully.

I looked up the shaft and could only make out the two lights beaming back down at me. They were only illuminating the first few feet of the shaft and I doubted they could see anything of me but my headlamp as I looked back up. The dirt and rock walls seemed to absorb the light, instead of reflecting it. Was that normal?

I took one more tentative step down and my rope ran out. I looked down, only to discover I had reached the last rung of the ladder and my foot was only inches from the dirt floor. I pulled on the rope to take the tension off my harness and lifted myself free of the rope. I gave the rope a couple of quick pulls.

"Okay! Come on down!" I yelled. My voice echoed up the shaft and down the tunnels to my left and right and ahead. This area seemed to be where a few systems came together. I guess that made sense. All tunnels leading to the exit was a good idea and I'm sure everyone who worked down here knew this labyrinth like the backs of their hands. Suddenly I had a little flash back to the gold tunnels in Egypt. Strange how long ago that was but how we still dug in the ground for the secrets it held. I suddenly felt a chill up my spine. Morah?

I saw the ladder wobble a bit and knew Jon or Nathan were on their way down. I stepped back just in case some rocks fell or the ladder flew apart.

Hopefully not because a body would come flying down.

"Looks like Jon is gonna be the rotten egg," I heard Nathan yell from above.

"Just go slow and easy. This ladder belongs in a museum!" I yelled back.

Finally, I saw his legs come through the hole in the ceiling as the rest of his body creeped down, inch by inch. Nathan was a tall drink of water to begin with so if the ladder held for him, it should hold for Jon. Maybe that was their line of thinking. Maybe they drew straws. I'd have to ask later.

"Okay, two down, one to go," I said to Nathan.

"If that stupid ladder wasn't in the way, we could practically repel down," he said.

"Yeah, but it might come in handy on the way back up. This crappy ladder will be better than nothing. At least I hope so, because climbing out with the rope alone will suck lemons," I said.
The ladder once again began to shake as Jon made his way down. Being shorter and lighter than either Nathan or I, Jon was down in half the time it took either of us.

"That was fun," he said, but without the smile. "Well, there are three tunnels here, and three of us, but if Scooby-Doo has taught us anything, it's never to split up, so who wants to pick our first tunnel to explore?" I asked.

"I vote on the Eeny Meeny methodology," I said.

"It's as good as any," Jon said with a smile.

"Eeny, meeny, miny, moe, catch a tiger by the toe, if he hollers, let it go, Eeny, meeny, miny, moe," I said, while pointing at each opening per word. We ended up with the opening to our right, which seemed as good as any.

We all turned on our headlamps to their brightest setting and pointed our tiny LED flashlights towards the hole in the wall as we started down its path. The smell of dirt and rock and mustiness was so thick, you could practically taste it. The walls and ceiling were shored up with large pieces of wood every few feet, but they felt inadequate for holding up the tons of rock and dirt over our heads. After a few minutes of walking, we came to the end but there was a hole in the ground and another ladder protruding.

"So, do we explore this mine per level or just keep going down?" Nathan asked.

"Jon, any thoughts?" I asked.

"If we keep backtracking every time we come to an end, we'll be here forever. Let's try to not cover the same ground more than once if we can help it," he said.

"Sounds like solid logic to me so down we go," I said.

Thankfully, this ladder looked completely sturdy. Maybe the first ladder was just a way to discourage people from going down if they happen to get the door open. If we hadn't had the ropes, I doubt we would have tried to descend so hopefully, the rest of our adventure didn't rely on antique ladders.

After we had all descended to the next level, we once again walked down a long tunnel, only to be met again by another hole and another ladder. Once again we descended to another level.

"Uh, how far underground do you suppose we are?" asked Nathan.

"Sixty? Seventy feet, maybe," Jon replied.

"I'm not claustrophobic but this feels really weird. Remind me not to sign up for the next spelunking tour you arrange," Nathan said.

"Jon, how are you holding up?" I asked.

"So far, so good, but I'm with Nathan. This feels really weird, almost like there is some vibration in the air. Do you feel it?" Jon asked.

We all stood quiet and still for a moment.

"Crap. Now that you mention it, I do hear or feel some vibration. I can't tell if my ears hear it or my skin feels it. Maybe both," I said.

"Well, let's keep trucking. Let's see if it gets stronger or weaker as we move down this tunnel," I said.

We walked for about three more minutes and once again came to another hole in the floor, and another ladder poking out but this time we stopped and listened again for the vibration.

"Okay, I definitely hear and feel it now and it seems to be coming from down there," Nathan said as we all pointed our flashlights into the hole.

But nothing happened. What I mean is, when we pointed our lights into the hole, we couldn't see into the hole. All we could see was the end of the ladder protruding from the hole and then blackness, like the hole was just a painted circle on the floor. Our lights didn't bounce off of the hole, it was more like our lights were absorbed by the hole.

"Ooooooooooooh. That's weird. Right?" I asked.

"Is there a hole there or is this some weird prop?" Nathan asked.

Jon took a couple of tentative steps towards the hole and grabbed the ladder. He gave it a push, and sure enough, it moved, just as if it went down a long hole, except we couldn't see beyond the blackness of the hole it went in to. It was like a cartoon hole except it was real and right in front of us.

I pulled off my pack and took out my last piece of rope. I tied one end to the top loop on the pack and walked over to the hole.

"Let's see what happens," I said.

As the pack touched and lowered into the hole, it became instantly enveloped by the blackness until it completely disappeared and all we could see was the rope. I continued to lower the pack another fifteen feet or so until I could feel the rope go slack.

"I guess I hit the bottom. I'll bring it back up, and hopefully there isn't some monster on the other end," I said with a smile.

"Not funny, man," Nathan said. I looked to Jon and I believe he seconded the motion.

I slowly pulled the pack back up and it eventually emerged, no worse the wear. It wasn't on fire or glowing or anything crazy. It was just my pack. I untied the rope and began to stow it back in the pack.

"Ok, who goes first? Eeny Meeny?" I asked with a grin.

37

Dung

Their voices faded as they left the large room to make their way to their eating hall. The motion of the ship had ceased but I was sure we were no longer on the ground. I wondered how Morah and Academ were going to critique my current situation.

My choices seemed extremely limited. If Gretimus was going to discuss his plan for the humans then that was the information I was going to need. If I didn't start following the crew to the eating hall, I had little hope of listening to them, because I was sure to become hopelessly lost. Time to move.

I checked the room one last time to ensure I was alone then sprinted to the other side where they had gone through another door and down a hall. I stopped and listened. I could barely make out the sounds of their conversations. This was just about as bad of a plan as I could imagine. All I could do is follow them at the safest distance possible, trying not to lose them before they entered the hall. At the same time, I had to hope I didn't run into some stray lizard coming down the hall or out of one of the many doors I saw before me on either side. There were more ways this could go wrong than go right but I had little choice.

The hallway curved to the right so I ran ahead, silent on bare feet, as I closed the distance between us enough that I could hear their voices much better. Mostly, it sounded like laughing, but a lizard's laugh was more of a cackling hiss, which was a bit unnerving. I still wasn't close enough to pick up their words. Hopefully, they wouldn't discuss their actual plans until they were eating. There was way too much hope built into this plan. I would need to revise my methods for making plans in the future. That was probably one of my many lessons I was sent here to learn.

When I had come close enough I could see their shadows, I slowed down and tried to stay just beyond their ability to look back to see me. Suddenly, the volume of their voices changed and I realized they must have left the hall. I peeked around the hallway to discover an open door they must have entered. I had no way of opening one of these doorways once they closed since there was no apparent device extending from the door. If I didn't go through that door before it closed, this entire trip would have been for nothing. I ran to the edge of the door and pressed my back to the wall. I could hear them still talking but their voices were moving away. Time seemed to be speeding up in my mind as I knew I probably only had some brief moments to act.

Not knowing exactly why, I got down on my hands and knees, took a deep breath, sent a silent thought to Morah, and quickly crawled through the door, staying close to the wall on the other side.

There was nowhere to hide. I was in the eating hall and all of the lizards were halfway across the room, walking away from me so no one was looking my way. Yet. I looked quickly left and right, trying to find any spot to conceal myself. Nothing. If just one of the four or five lizards turned around, they were going to see an earth boy staring back at them. The only cover was straight ahead, behind one of the many tables the lizards had already walked past but still a distance that seemed oceans away. I guess when you're presented with only one option, the decision is easy.

Moving as cautiously and slowly as possible, I tried to move forward and hide behind a table before someone caught my movement. My heart was about to pound out of my chest and I could hardly hear them talking from the pounding in my ears. Thank goodness my feet weren't sweating as much as my hands were. I'd be leaving a trail of water if they were.

Just as they reached the front table, I came to a stop at the first table I was able to reach. It didn't provide complete cover from being seen but if I stayed low enough, I might stay out of their direct sight. As they sat, Gretimus began yelling for someone to bring the food before he had to grind them into some kind of lump. Some of his words did not make sense. I tried to calm myself so I could listen to what they were saying. I took a few long, deep breaths to get my heart rate back down to normal.

"Gretimus, my old friend, how in the name of Stumus do you think you can get this human situation under control?" one of the lizards said.

"The problem with the humans is this," Gretimus began. "Of all of the races we have encountered and dominated throughout the galaxy, humans have evolved faster and adapted to their environment quicker than any other, by many magnitudes. They live hundreds of their own years as well, which I believe adds to the problem. If they had shorter life spans, they would not learn as quickly and advance as far in such a short period of time. If we allow them to go unchecked, they may very well advance beyond even our own technology one day and become a power to equal or surpass our own. We cannot allow this!"

"Fine," said the lizard across the table from him, "but we can't change the lifespans of all of those humans. Even if we knew how, there are too many of them for us to change and they breed too quickly. It would take an army of us generations just to change a fraction of them. But this is moot because we cannot do these things."

"Correct!" said Gretimus.

"So how do we change that?" he asked, waiting for someone to answer.

"You fools, the answer is simple!" he said, sounding triumphant in his plan.

"We kill the humans!" he blurted out, in his hiss of a language.

There was a long pause of silence.

"Gretimus, if we kill all of the humans, who will supply our gold? Did we not allow them to flourish so we could use their labor?" he asked.

"We will not kill all of them!" he yelled, or hissed. I could hardly tell the difference with the lizards. "We will kill most of them but leave enough that we can change the life spans of the few who remain. Those who breed afterwards will promote the limited life span as well. Problem solved."

"How do you propose we accomplish this?" his friend asked. "We do not possess the crew or firepower to destroy so many."

"Did I not tell you I had a plan?!" he bellowed as loudly as I had ever heard a lizard hiss.

"We shall return to the planet and visit many different communities. We shall tell them that we are unhappy with them and soon, a great flood will destroy the world. We will tell them to build structures or find the highest ground to survive the coming wrath from the gods. When sufficient time has passed, we will flood their world and the few who remain will be changed," he said, with what I could only describe as a hiss of satisfaction.

"Brilliant! Now we have the ability to flood entire planets and change life spans! You are a genius, Gretimus! Let us all celebrate our friend who has the best brain in the galaxy!" the lizard to his left said.

Without a hint of warning, Gretimus immediately punched the other lizard, who fell from his seat with a thud and stayed on the floor with his eyes shut.

"Any other critiques of my plan?" Gretimus asked.

"Gretimus, please first explain to your less brilliant crew how you plan to flood the planet," the one across the table asked.

"We have the ability to tow space rock with our ship," he said.

"True," his friend agreed.

"We will tow several chunks of rock into their orbit and position them to strike both of their poles. This will cause the ice to melt, earthquakes to ensue and create enough water to vaporize to produce rain for days. Whoever is left afterwards can be gathered and changed," Gretimus beamed.

"One last question, my leader," his friend said, with maybe a hint of lizard sarcasm.

"Yes?" he asked, ready to fly across the table at his crewmate.

"Who exactly will be gathering those remaining humans and changing them? I have not heard that we possess such a technology," he asked.

"Oh, I have made a very special alliance with another race who have been looking to use this planet for their own purposes but will not hamper or hinder ours. They are masters at these kinds of things," he said, rather proud of himself.

Just then, the lizard who had been knocked to the floor decided to open his eyes. He was staring straight at me. Dung.

38

Way Down Under

"It's my mission, I'll go first," I said. They both instantly looked relieved. I couldn't blame them. Going into a magical black cartoon hole didn't seem like a great plan and if Karen were here, I bet there would be more discussion but we were wasting time and this was obviously the place we were looking for.

"Okay, don't laugh, but I'm going to stick my pinky finger into the hole and if it doesn't dissolve or catch on fire, I'll head on down," I said. A backpack was one thing, but my skin was something else and who knew what this really was.

Slowly, with Jon and Nathan watching me, I inserted my left pinky finger into the hole. Nothing. It didn't feel any different. No pain, no different sensation. It was just as if the hole wasn't there. I pulled my finger back out and it was still in one piece. I flexed it a couple of times, just to prove it still worked. We all looked at each other with a sigh of relief.

"Look, if I go down there and there is a bunch of alien eggs with face suckers inside, I'm coming back up this ladder screaming," I said, half-joking.

"Are you trying to scare the crap out of me? Because you're doing an awesome job!" Nathan said with a straight face.

"Okay, here goes nothing," I said as I grabbed the top of the ladder and swung myself around to put my foot on the first rung to go down.

I watched my foot and then my leg disappear into the inky blackness of the hole, still with absolutely no effect. This was some interesting technology that I hoped we could somehow figure out and use for ourselves one day, but for now, I just needed to get down this ladder.

I slowly went down, step by step, until only my head protruded above the hole.

"I bet this looks pretty weird," I said.

"Please just go, it looks like a decapitated head and you're freaking me out," Jon said.

"See ya on the other side," I said, hoping they'd enjoy the play on words. They didn't.

I took one more step and disappeared into total blackness. Total. I looked down, but there was nothing. It was as if I was enveloped in tar but could move freely. I couldn't see Jon or Nathan above me, even though I knew they had their headlamps and flashlights beaming at the hole.

I reached up to turn my headlamp on only to remember it was already on but not producing any light. I pulled my small LED flashlight from my pocket and clicked the end to turn it on. Nothing. Either light did not emit here or the hole disabled electronics. I decided to take a step up and let Jon and Nathan know this development.

I took a step up and popped my head out of the hole only to be met by both of them giving a little scream. It was kind of funny but I had to imagine they just saw a head with no body attached popping out of a hole. We'd laugh about this later. Hopefully.

"What the hell, man!" Nathan said.

"Sorry, but I needed to let you know that our lights don't work down here so don't be too freaked out when you don't have any light. When I get to the bottom and want you to come down, I'll shake the ladder a bit. Okay?" I said.

"Yeah, just don't pop your head back up like that, it's fucking creepy!" Jon said. Jon didn't drop the F bomb very often so it must be pretty fucking creepy.

I popped my head back down and began my slow, step by step descent into the ink. With every step I took, the vibration in the air increased. I knew I only had about twenty feet to go down if the pack was any indication, so one way or another, this wasn't going to take very long. However, I wasn't sure if my ears or body could withstand the increasing intensity of the vibrating. I just wanted to plug my ears with my fingers but I needed to hold onto the ladder. The air itself seemed to be moving so much, I was afraid my entire body was going to shake apart before I reached the bottom. Just as I was about to abandon the descent, my foot touched the floor and the vibrations instantly stopped but an explosion of light took its place.

Going from total darkness to blinding white light instantaneously was unnerving. I'd be lying if I didn't admit I gave out a little yelp. It certainly caught me off-guard.

For a few seconds, I couldn't see anything as my eyes tried to adjust to the light. I tried to blink and shield my eyes quickly to attempt to see my surroundings. If I was about to step into a big alien egg, I wanted to be back up that ladder pronto.

Slowly, my eyes adjusted and I could see I was in a large, domed, metallic room. It was easily fifty feet high in the center and the walls were completely smooth. They were a mixture of silver and gold and as you looked around, the color seemed to shift so that you weren't really sure what color it actually was. Weird.

My ladder protruded from the very edge of the dome and went into its ceiling. Our last tunnel must come to the very edge of the dome walls to be able to be this high. One thing was for sure: miners in the late 1800s and early 1900s did not build this room.

As my eyes continued to adjust, I could tell there were areas in the walls near the floors that were probably doors but they were closed and showed no exterior hardware to suggest an obvious way to open them. I'd seen this trick before so that didn't concern me so much.

Knowing that Jon and Nathan were probably beginning to get worried, I gave the ladder a good shake, wondering which one would be brave/stupid enough to follow me down here next. The decision was who wants to be brave enough to go into the black hole of nothing versus who wants to be left in the creepy tunnel alone.

A few seconds later I saw Jon's legs coming through the hole in the ceiling. At least he would have the luxury of light when he came down the last bit. I noticed that this end of the hole in the ceiling did the same trick as the top part, so he was probably in the blackness for a few feet before exiting the hole. Thankfully, he didn't have to endure the bone-shattering vibrations. That must have been some type of deterrent. It nearly worked.

"Welcome to the Thunder Dome!" I said, trying to add some levity to the situation.

"Wow, this just went from weird to crazy," Jon said. I had to agree but I could tell this was built by one of our friends in the stars, not by humans.

A few seconds later, Nathan's body emerged from the hole and he gave a whistle as his foot hit the floor.

"I guess we're not in Kansas anymore," he said.

"At least there's no alien eggs or face-huggers down here," I said.

"Yet," Jon said.

We all looked at each other. Truthfully, I'd seen several aliens in my lives and travels and none looked like the xenomorph from Alien. At least so far. Since I preferred my underwear stain-free, I hoped I never ran into one in the future. Near or otherwise.

"Who built this?" Nathan asked to no one in particular.

"I have a good idea but let's investigate and see what we can turn up. We still have a few hours before we need to meet the car," I said.

We began randomly walking around the dome. There was absolutely nothing here but the floor, the ladder into the ceiling, and the four doors spaced equally around the walls which we had no idea how to open.

Jon and Nathan walked to the doors and I began to walk to the center of the room. As I approached the center, a silver pedestal soundlessly emerged from the floor as if it were growing from the floor itself. When it reached about waist height, the end began to enlarge until it was an orb about the size of a softball. Then it just stopped. I was standing about three feet away from it and decided not moving was my best course of action at the moment.

I looked at Jon and Nathan to see if they had witnessed what just happened. I knew alien ships had this type of technology on it but I didn't really expect it here. There was no telling what this did. Was this used for defense? Communication? Deathray? I didn't see any instructions or markings. The orb and pedestal were shiny and completely smooth.

"Uh......should we move?" Nathan asked.

"No idea but we can't stand here forever either," I said and took a step towards the object.

Nothing happened. So I took one more step, which put me inches away from the orb. Still nothing. No sound, no ray, no lights.

"I guess you can come closer," I said, giving them the option to choose their own fate.

They looked at each other across the room like a western shootout, waiting for the other one to make a move. I almost laughed when they both took a step at the exact same time, like it was choreographed. A few seconds later, we all stood around the object, looking at it as if it might do a trick any second.

"Any suggestions," Jon asked.

"Oh, mighty orb! Can you tell us why you are here?" I said in a goofy voice.

For a second, we waited to see if anything actually happened. Then we all smiled.

"Hey, it was worth a shot, right?" I half-laughed.

Without thinking, I casually reached out and put my hand on the top of the orb and said....

"Really, I wonder what the hell.......

Suddenly, I was in a ship. It looked familiar, but not like I had actually been here. I had seen something similar in the past. Somewhere. But there were people around me. Well, they were kind of people. There were four of them. They had pale skin and white hair. They almost looked angelic, at least from a human perspective. There was no way to tell if they were male or female or something in between but they looked flawlessly beautiful.

These were the Pleiadians! Morah had taken me on one of his field trips long ago to visit these advanced race of beings. We had only studied them very briefly. They were not a threat to Earth but they were known to visit occasionally so Morah thought it a good idea to know who they were if I should ever encounter them. Today was that day. But what drew my attention was the necklace one of them was wearing. It was THE necklace! But things weren't going so well for them at the moment. They were in a panic.

No one seemed to notice me and I had the same feeling as when I was a disembodied soul watching scenes play before me.

"Our field has been damaged! We can no longer leave this planet's gravity or even stay above it much longer!" one of them said as he ran from one part of the room to the other, apparently checking instruments I did not completely understand.

"Why are they shooting at us?!" another one said, apparently scared and exasperated.

Suddenly the room pitched sideways violently, apparently from an explosion of some type and everyone grabbed whatever they could to keep from being thrown across the room.

"Internal gravity dampers are destroyed! We need to land immediately or we are going to crash!" the first one yelled.

They all seemed scared and upset, which I could completely understand. But where was I and how did I get here? It was as if I were in "soul" form again.

"Land at the planet's southern pole and use whatever deflectors we have left to get as far under the surface as we can. Hopefully, we can hide our ship there until we can make repairs," said the second one.

For a few moments they were all busy, trying to carry out the orders.

I watched a screen that seemed suspended in the air as a three-dimensional representation of the earth appeared. It showed several dots appear over the planet. Three of the dots were red and one was blue. I felt the reds ones represented the aliens who were hunting this ship. The blue dot must represent this ship. It was heading for what appeared to be the South Pole. The closer we got, the more detailed the 3-D map appeared to become.

"I have found a suitable spot but we must act immediately. The Draconians may pinpoint our location at any moment," a third one said.

We advanced at an amazing speed towards the ice and snow ahead of us. I could tell they were all feeling the acceleration, as they seemed to be bracing for an impact.

"Convert all energy to shields and let the ship travel as far as possible into the ice," the first one said.

They all glanced at each other for a moment, checking to see if they all agreed that this was a good idea, but they seemed to silently agree there were no other options.

Suddenly, they hit the ice. The ship bounced around so fiercely it threatened to break into pieces. Each of the four were hopelessly thrown around the room like rag dolls until finally, the ship had come to a silent rest. No smoke or fire or beeping noises. Everything was silent and still.

Slowly, with much groaning, each of the four emerged from where they had been thrown. The ship was sitting at an angle, so the floor was no longer level. They held onto pieces of chairs and panels to move back to the center of the room.

"Is anyone hurt?" the first on asked.

Everyone seemed to consider this for a moment, but no one spoke.

"Ptaah, did the Draconians track our location?" the one who seemed to be in charge asked.

"Standby," Ptaah said. He seemed to be checking several different instruments with a somewhat frustrated look on his face.

"Sfath, some of our instruments have suffered damage, but it appears none of the Draconian ships are in our area so it seems they do not currently know our whereabouts," Ptaah said.

They all took a moment to breathe a sigh of relief.

"As soon as we are sure they have not tracked us, we will begin to make repairs," Sfath said.

Suddenly, the scene changed and I was no longer inside of the ship. I was standing in a gigantic cavern that appeared to be made of ice and the ship was in the center of this cave. Two of the men were holding some square instruments but neither looked happy as they stared at the ship from several feet away. I felt as if some time had passed since the last scene I had witnessed.

"There is simply no way to finish repairs," said the first on. "The magnetic field cannot be properly established without equipment. That equipment does not exist on this planet, and there is no way to contact anyone without the field being generated. We are stuck here."

A voice came out of the ship as Sfath walked down a ramp extended from the ship.

"Our supplies are nearly depleted. This was never meant to be an extended mission so we have perhaps six of this planets cycles left before they are gone. I believe our best option is to take our lander and attempt to establish a secondary base of operations as far away from this ship as possible," Sfath said.

"Where do you propose we establish this base?" one of the others asked.

"From previous scouting reports the area best adapted to match Pleiades sets here," Sfath said as a three-dimensional globe appeared above his outstretched hand. It increased in size and then seemed to zoom into a specific area, which I immediately recognized. I had been studying this same area for months. It was Leadville, Colorado.

"We can use the lander to dig out a large enough base beneath the surface that the Draconians will not be able to detect us. The area shows little to no indigenous life that would threaten us. We could easily make our own food there with its available resources and stay until we

determine a way to fix our ship, are found by our
brothers, or die," he said.
They all looked at each other as if they knew
which option would come to be.

I was staring at Jon and Nathan, as I quickly
pulled my hand from the orb.

"Crap! Did you see that too?!" I blurted out.

"See what?" Jon asked.

I looked at both of them in disbelief. I had been
gone for what seemed like fifteen minutes in total.
Didn't they realize that I wasn't there, or I had
zoned out for a while?

"For the last several minutes, I was on board an
alien ship. I believe it's the ship we're looking for
and I know where it is and what this place is," I
said quicker than I meant to. I tried to slow down.

"Did you ever see that Star Trek episode where
Picard blacks out and lives an entire lifetime, only
to return to the Enterprise where everyone thinks
he was only unconscious for a few moments?" I
said.

They just stared at each other.

"Come on, guys! Not one Trekkie here?" I
asked, kind of seriously.

"Should we try to open any of the doors?"
Nathan asked.

"We still have some time left so let's give it a
shot," I said.

We each walked to a separate door but as I approached mine, I couldn't see any type of device that would open the door. Only the faint outline of the door itself was visible. I put my hand on the door and thought *open* but nothing happened. Then I said *open* out loud. Nothing. I turned to look at the other guys who were actually watching my failed attempts.

Jon turned to his door and just knocked. I started laughing but we all waited for a few moments to see if someone answered.

Nothing.

"It was a good try," I said. "Okay, Nathan, that leaves you."

Nathan walked back to the center of the room and put his hand on the orb and closed his eyes. I began to wonder if he was experiencing the same scenes I had earlier but suddenly all four of the doors opened.

Nathan opened his eyes and smiled.

"How did you do that?" Jon asked.

"I just thought *open all of the doors*, and when I opened my eyes, they were open," he said.

"Cool," I said. "Okay, Jon and I will go investigate. Nathan, stay here and if these doors close, keep opening them so we don't get stuck on the other side. Jon, let's do this together"
I walked over to Jon's door, looked back at Nathan, and took a step inside. Jon waited about half a second to follow me. Probably making sure

I didn't explode or disappear. I couldn't blame him.

We had only gone a few feet before we were inside another room shaped like the first one, except one third the size. It was equally empty. I only imagined that it held a variety of hidden instruments or furnishings which only materialized when called to do so. I walked to the center of the room to see if another orb appeared but nothing happened this time. Maybe you needed the necklace or mind control abilities to make the rest of the facility work properly. We had neither, so no need to hang around.

"Let's check out another door," I said, and Jon made his way to the main room.

When we emerged, Nathan looked a bit relieved.

"Nothing but an empty room, we'll see what's behind door number two," I said. Jon rolled his eyes.

Again, we found a small room but this one held a surprise. Built into the walls were long shelves with what appeared to be glass viewing doors but without a visible way to open them. As we approached them, we discovered what became of the occupants of the ship.

Each shelf held a body but it was obvious that they had died eons ago. They appeared human, but each had blond hair, and was taller than the average human. They each wore the same clothing that I saw in the flashback. They obviously never found a way to fix their ship.

I looked around their necks to see if any of them possessed a necklace similar to the one Baby Doe had worn in the painting but none did.

"I guess they didn't have that pod technology to put themselves into sleep until they could be rescued," Jon said.

"Yeah, guess not. Let's go check out the other doors," I said.

As we came out, I yelled out to Nathan, "Four dead dudes," which made his eyes twice the size.

We walked into number three and immediately thought we had hit the jackpot. A ship! It was tiny, about the size of a Blackhawk helicopter but it was definitely their ship. There was no mistaking the classic smooth, long silver, orb-like structure.

"This must have been the one they used to get here from the South Pole," I said, forgetting I hadn't told Jon or Nathan the flashback story yet.

Jon just gave me a quizzical look.

"I'll explain later. Let's see if we can figure out how to get inside," I said.

After a good fifteen minutes, we had yet to find any way to get into the ship. There wasn't even a place where a door was outlined. There was nothing else in the room to give a hint as to how the ship opened, operated, or even managed to get into this domed cavern. It was time to give up and perhaps try again later. Nathan must be getting worried by now.

"Let's regroup with Nathan and hit the road since we don't want to be late for our ride. Hopefully we can come back if need be," I said.

"Sounds good," Jon said.

When we came back out of the door, Nathan looked happy to see us.

"What took you so long? I was starting to think the face-huggers had eaten you," he said, but only half-joking.

"We found the small ship they used to come here from the South Pole. Okay, let's get out of here and I'll tell you both the entire story on the way," I said.

As soon as Jon and Nathan made their way up the ladder, I took off my spare Road ID, synced its hidden chip with my Garmin watch and then laid it at the base of the pedestal. No sense in taking any chances with this information. The term *once bitten, twice shy*, came to mind.

As we made our way back out, I gave them the entire story. They asked a few questions but I told them to hold off until we got back to the house so we could ask all of our questions together and not repeat ourselves.

We reached the last ladder and Jon was first up, since he was the lightest and had the best odds of actually making it up without destroying the rickety old relic. When he reached the top, we heard him say something but he was so far away, it was only a muffled sound.

I told Nathan to go up second. I'd bring up the rear and if I needed to be pulled up, I'd rather have him there to help Jon. He started up the ladder, using as much of the ropes and the wall as possible to take the weight off the ladder.

When he got about halfway up, a few pieces of the rungs came crashing down but not the entire thing. Hopefully there would be some of the ladder left for my turn.

Eventually, the rope stopped moving. I assumed he made it and it was my turn. Again, I heard some noises from above but couldn't make out what was being said.

My turn. As carefully as I could, I pulled myself up, putting small amounts of my weight on the outside of each rung, while trying to keep my opposite foot on the wall to steady myself. Most of my weight was on the rope and after twenty feet, I was getting pretty tired but knew I only had a short distance to go. I wondered why no one was looking over the edge to see where I was. Finally, I pulled myself up and out of the hole, a little miffed no one was there to give me a handout.

When I turned around I saw the problem.

Steve was pointing a device at Jon and Nathan, both of whom had their hands up in the classic "*I give up*" stance. Steve looked like the cat who just ate the canary. Apparently, lizards have nine lives too.

39

Home

He screamed like only an alien lizard can. At that point, I knew I was had. I was on a spaceship that was actually in space. No matter where I ran, I'd only be putting off the inevitable. I simply stood up and waited to see what happened next.

"Seize him!" Gretimus barked at no one and everyone in the room.

I didn't try to run or hide. I simply stood and waited to be seized. I had to remember not to appear to understand what they were saying. I needed to treat them as if they were gods, not alien lizards.

"Who are you and how did you get on this ship?" Gretimus thundered at me.

He was speaking his native language so I pretended not to understand. Was this a test or did he simply forget that earthling Egyptians could not understand his language? He looked back and forth between his crew as if they might be able to answer for me.

"Answer me you fool or you will die a painful death!" he bellowed.

"Gretimus, he cannot understand you. Speak his language," his brave friend reminded him.

He looked flustered, as if this was far beneath him to waste his time on. I fully expected to be smashed in the face, just like the crewmate who questioned him earlier. I simply averted my eyes towards the floor, like a good little Egyptian should.

After a few moments, he finally began speaking to me in Egyptian.

"How did you come to be on this ship, boy?" he asked.

"I came to load a cask of beer but could find no one about. I came inside to seek assistance and when I heard you coming back, I became frightened and hid inside. I am so sorry, great Set. I live only to please you. Please allow me to go back to my service with the priests so we can continue to gather your gold and prepare for your future visits," I begged, hoping he would believe me. Honestly, I was only half acting.

"What shall we do with him, Gretimus?" his second-in-command asked.

"He has seen too much. He cannot be allowed to report what he has witnessed to his people. Take him to the lock and let him taste the heavens that his people worship so much," Gretimus said as easily as if he were ordering a drink of wine.

"Wouldn't he make an excellent servant for us while we traveled?" the one who received the punch asked.

"You fool. He would be twice the burden as half the help. Take him away immediately before I decide you will join him!" he snorted.

"Yes, mighty Gretimus," he said. Did I detect a bit of sarcasm?

The one who tried to save me came to my side and grabbed my arm, as another one did the same to my other side. They lifted me up high enough so that my toes barely touched the floor. We spun around and began to march towards the door I had slipped through moments ago.

There was no fighting these monsters. I was much smaller and, up to this point, had never acquired any types of skills that would allow me to escape my current situation. I would have to rectify that in the future but I felt the sand slipping away from this life with every step they took forward.

"I believe we could have used him for all of the menial tasks Gretimus has us perform on this luxury ship," the punched one stated to his friend.

"I would keep that opinion and ones like it to yourself in the future, unless you enjoy having your snout flattened on a regular basis," his companion said.

That received only a grunt as a reply.

Two turns later and we were standing at a fairly large door. It was dirty, and the area had smells that were foreign to me. Maybe this is what all ships smelled like. I had no comparison. However, I knew that the other side of the door was not a place I wanted to be.

Smashed snout hit a colored disc next to the door and it made a harsh sound as it opened. I was instantly shoved forward into the room. The door quickly shut again to lock me inside. I didn't pound on the door or cry or act frightened. Doing so would only mean I understood my immediate situation and may hamper my mission in the future.

The lizards looked through the small window in the door. I think they were disappointed by my lack of fear. They spoke words to each other that I could not hear and then loud noises began to fill the room. I was curious as to how dying would feel and was prepared for the experience but my rapid heartbeat gave me away and I knew I was frightened. I wondered why.

Out of the corner of my eye, a light began to shine in the corner of the room. It slowly took the shape of Academ! I thought I must be seeing things but Academ simply smiled at me.

"Why are you here Academ?" I asked. I was happy to see my teacher, but confused as to why she was here right now.

"Timlis, there is no need for you to experience the pain of this death. That is not part of your mission. I have come to take you before this body dies," she said.

"Would it be a painful death?" I asked.

"Yes," she said back.

All this time, both lizards continued to watch me while I had this conversation with a soul they could not see. I imagined they believed I was praying to the gods.

As the doors at the far end of the room began to open, I could feel the pressure of the room begin to change. Suddenly, I felt a lightness that my mind remembered but my body had forgotten as an infant. I traveled upward, like a breeze had caught me and whisked me away. I felt free of gravity and as I looked down, I could see my human body being pulled quickly through the opened doors and outside of the ship. I looked so small. I wondered at the pain I could no longer feel.

"Are you ready?" Academ asked.

"Ready? Ready for what?" I asked.

"Ready to go home," she said with happiness.

"Let us go home," I said.

A cloudy tunnel slowly formed before us as we began to be pulled gently inside. I could feel as much as hear a gentle hum and chime that seemed to be the source of the tunnel. It was as if it were pulling us along. I felt the burdens of my life as Sabaf begin to melt away as we continued along the tunnel, the light of my soul pushed against Academ's as we made our short journey. Home.

40

Loose Ends

I am pretty slow to anger but Steve was starting to wear me thin in that department. How many times did I have to shoot this guy and slice him in half before he died or got the message to stop pestering me? But now he was pointing a nasty looking weapon at two of my friends and it was time to make sure that didn't happen again.

Unfortunately, I had no way of knowing if fork-tongued Steve had reported his location back to his buddies above. It was a chance I couldn't take. I slowly put my hands behind my back and touched the side buttons on my Garmin watch. This wouldn't take very long.

"I think we have some unfinished business, Jim," he said, using my actual name.

"You seem to have me at several disadvantages, Steve, but since our last encounter, I don't think that's your real name either," I said, trying to buy us enough time until my distraction took effect.

"Names aren't really important here but since I know you and your foolish friends will keep this secret, my name is Hordius," he said, clearly indicating he intended to kill us soon.

"So, Hordius, what is it exactly that you want from us?" I asked.

"You can stop your charade, Jim. I know you are looking for the ship. I know that the Pleiadians hid that ship and they never left this planet. They obviously hid themselves until they died on this wretched outpost of a rock and I think you may have found their little hiding hole. You have information and you are going to give it to me. All three of you are going back down that hole and you are going to show me exactly what you found," he said, obviously feeling pretty confident.

"What makes you think you can get us to take you down some dusty tunnels?" I asked, pushing my luck just a bit.

"You're right, Jim. Three of you are too hard to keep track of. Time to increase my odds," he said as he pointed the gun at Nathan.

Just then the timer on my Garmin must have hit zero. The ground under our feet shook as a well-placed explosion went off under our feet. As the tunnels began to collapse, the entire area began to shift up and down.

"Hey, lizard breath," I said. "I don't think anyone is going into those tunnels unless you have some earth moving equipment stashed around here somewhere. In fact, if we don't move away from here pronto, I think we might become permanent parts of this museum," I said, as we could feel the ground under our feet continue to shift.

"No matter, all I have to do it take you back to the ship and pull your tiny brain apart until I find what I want. These other two are of no use to me," he said, waving his weapon between the two of them.

"What makes you think I'm the one who knows where the ship is?" I asked.

This made him hesitate for a moment. Clearly he hadn't thought this through.

"Only one of us knows the location so you have some bad odds against you here," I said.

"As they are so fond of saying on this planet, bullshit," he said. "You are the leader here, so you clearly have the information. Time to go, Jim; say goodbye to your friends," he sneered.

Just as he pointed the shiny weapon at Nathan, Hordius's head exploded. For a moment, his body stood straight, arm still extended, as if it was unaware that it was missing its head, but then he crumpled to the ground.

We looked at each other, and then noticed some movement in the darkness, behind Hordius's now crumpled body. Sid was still holding a rather large handgun, pointing to where our lizard acquaintance had just been standing. Karen was standing just behind her.

"I don't think he'll be slicing off anyone else's feet for quite some time," Sid said. She had a look of satisfaction on her face. I couldn't blame her. If anyone deserved to blow this alien's head off, it was Sid.

"Yeah, I think his feet slicing days have come to an end," I added, just as the ground under our feet began to shift and sway.

"Someone help me dump what's left of this bastard down the hole before the entire place collapses under our feet," I said.

All around us, large swaths of ground were collapsing forty or fifty feet at a time, causing thunderous sounds to erupt from the holes opening in the ground. This had to be echoing all over the area and it was only a matter of time until someone started investigating.

Nathan grabbed Hordius's feet as Jon and I each grabbed an arm. We drug him to the entrance to the mine and tossed him in, neck first. I closed the hatch and pulled an old lock from my backpack. I quickly attached the lock and started towards Sid and Karen.

"Hopefully, that's the last time I have to drop that bastard down a dark hole," I said, slightly out of breath.

"Why put a lock back on?" Nathan asked as we started running away from the mine.

"Just in case anyone investigates, they'll see a lock still attached to the door. I doubt there will be any mine left to go into but at least they might not think someone actually blew it up. Hopefully they will just think it's a collapse," I said.

More of the ground around us began to vibrate and shift as the tunnels beneath us continued to collapse. I looked back to see Baby Doe's house fall in on itself as the ground swallowed it whole. The dust and dirt was getting as thick as fog. It was getting tough to breathe in the already thin air. We all ran faster, following Karen and Sid.

"How far to the car?!" I yelled.

"About 200 more yards!" Karen yelled as she kicked it into high gear, apparently motivated by the minor earthquake I had caused.

"Did YOU do this?!" Sid yelled as we ran shoulder to shoulder down the dirt road.

"Yup, I couldn't leave what we found for someone else to discover," I said.

"Maybe you could have waited until we were a bit further away to blow the place up!" Karen yelled, making it more of a statement than a question.

Finally, as we reached the car, the ground stopped shaking. Karen jumped in the driver's seat, Sid shotgun, the three of us stuffed in the back seat.

"Drive it like you stole it!" I yelled.

"Time to test out that rental insurance! Hang on, boys!" Karen yelled to us over her shoulder as she jammed the car into drive and smashed the gas pedal.

We began bouncing down the rocky dirt road, leaving a bit of carnage behind. I'm sure she didn't hit every single pothole and rock there was but she didn't miss many either. One of Leadville's historic icons was in ruins but now we knew why Baby Doe had never given up on the Matchless Mine and why it was locked up to the public.

The pieces of the puzzle were coming together. As glad as I was that pesky Steve/Hordius was out of the picture, I was sure he would be missed by someone. How he found us was also a problem because if Steve could find me, maybe some of his friends could, too. I'd just have to cross that bridge when I came to it.

For now, it was time to blend back in and look like the running team we were supposed to be. No more extra trips. No more bombs or aliens. Just boring old Jim, running a race and being helped by his friends. Move along, nothing special to see here folks.

EPILOGUE

The race went as planned. I ran 100 miles and barely finished before the 30 hour cut off time. I won't bore you with the details. My race report is public and well documented at BeginnerTriathlete. Suffice to say that we looked like a group of friends who came to Leadville for a race and that's how we looked when we left.

For a time, it appeared that we all went back to our daily lives. However, Sid came into some money that a long-lost relative had left her and she was able to buy herself a nifty new aircraft that could easily hold twelve people and any special equipment interesting world travelers might need. Some people are just lucky that way.

Over the next few months, the details of the next mission were carefully put together. More pieces of the puzzle found. Money moved. Properties bought. Plans made.

As I drove home from my I.T. job in Erlanger, I looked out my car window during a thunderstorm, my mind began to drift. I wondered if Morah and Academ approved of my antics. Just then, a bolt of lightning crashed on hundred feet from the edge of the road with a deafening explosion of thunder. I could only smile.

Congratulations! You made it to the end and hopefully you are looking forward to finding out what happened next. Good news! I'm hard at work on the next book and if you happened to have picked this up hot off the press, the next saga shouldn't be far behind. Just keep checking back on my Facebook page (Jim White, author) for updates. If you want to help spread the word, a Amazon review wouldn't hurt my feelings either. Hope you enjoyed this ride, and stay tuned for the next installment.

Atlantis!

Made in the USA
Monee, IL
31 August 2020